Banks of the Edisto:

A Journey In Time

Martha Clayton Banfield

Copyright © 2017 Martha Clayton Banfield

All rights reserved.

ISBN:1479335991

ISBN-13: 978-1479335992

No part of this publication may be reproduced, stored in a retrieval system, or transmitted in any form by any means, electronic, mechanical, photocopy, recording, or otherwise, without prior written permission of the author, except for brief quotations in critical reviews or articles.

DEDICATION

This book is dedicated to all of my Native American ancestors, as well as all of my German-Scott-Irish/English ancestors. This book is also for all who love history, and strive to keep history alive for everyone else. Although I have chosen to present this book as a fiction work, the background for it is based on actual historic facts, although names have been changed.

To all of those who spend countless hours in researching genealogy and doing the hard work of preserving the lineage and history of our ancestors, I commend you all, because I would not have had this story without the historic accounts of early South Carolinians, which were compiled by SC State Historian A. S. Salley, Jr., from earlier narratives by those who wrote it down, so that we can all learn from our past.

However, there is so much history that was not written down, but which the Lord allowed me to find and consider as background for this book. I have tried to keep the true heart of the Native Americans in mind as I wrote the book, and I believe the Holy Spirit has given me words for this book, as well as sent someone to help with the authenticity of the Native American way of life.

I have chosen to publish a fictional book so that I might have the liberty to take what some might consider *"boring"* old history, and make it come alive in the reader's mind. If it takes a modern day fictional story plot for us to learn of our history, then so be it; that is exactly what I have done.

Remember that the past is the road that we all must walk upon to get to the future. There is a message for everyone in this story, and I pray that those who read this book will feel the *"heart"* of this story.

CONTENTS

Acknowledgment

1 The Journey — Pg1
2 The Branch — Pg 27
3 The Book — Pg 59
4 Black Water — Pg 77
5 Edistowe Village — Pg 91
6 Waking Up — Pg 105

ACKNOWLEDGMENTS

I would like to acknowledge my son Michael Oglesby, who seems to just have the *"touch"* for finding Native American artifacts. From the time he was very small, he always had an eye for finding sharks teeth and other various artifacts.

Of course, that should be no surprise to me, since he has Cherokee from my own father's side of the family *(Gerald Clayton)* and Croatan Indian from his father's side. *(Betty Smith)* I guess he got a double dose of Native American blood, and the artifacts seem to *"call"* out to him to find.

I would also like to acknowledge those Native Americans who died while walking the trail of tears. America truly owes a great debt to the Native Americans, a debt which can not ever be repaid. Wrongs were committed, and although we cannot go back into the past and right them now, we can do what we can to honor the memory and legacy of the Native Americans who walked and lived in this nation before the white man came.

So, to my Native American ancestors, I pay tribute and honor to you all. Also, to my white English ancestors, I pay tribute to the ones who did not dishonor the Native Americans.

I would also like to make note that I have chosen to add EXTRA spaces between each paragraph, to make it easier for those who are vision impaired, to read this book. I also chose to BOLD all of the book itself, for easier reading.

CHAPTER 1- THE JOURNEY BEGINS

It was a beautiful sunny day near Bamberg, South Carolina. The air seemed uncannily alive, with a soft breeze blowing gently in the bright green leaves of the oak and gum trees in my back yard. I suddenly felt the urge to drive down to the Edisto River, which is the local blackwater river not far from my home.

I glanced at my Bible in the backseat of my car as I got into the front seat, glad that it was where it was supposed to be and where I had quick access to it. I also noticed that I still had the *"History of Bamberg South Carolina"* book in my back seat. I also saw the small basket which held some of my son's Native American artifacts, and which he had found and dearly treasured.

Suffice it to say, my son just had a knack for finding artifacts. Let me rephrase that-artifacts seemed to find my SON, he did not find them. Now I was ready to go, I thought to myself, armed with the Bible, the Bamberg County History book, and some Native American artifacts-arrowheads and pieces of pottery. I gingerly tossed my purse into the passenger seat beside me, and sped away, heading for *"Bobcat Landing."*

I just needed to get to the *"water."* Most anyone will understand just what I mean. That primordial need that lives inside of us-to be near the water, any kind of water; be it river, lake, pond, or ocean, just get me to the water! We humans just seem to need to *"get to the water"* where our minds can be eased with the ebb and flow of the waters. Some say that water mimics the water in a mother's womb, and so it comforts us; but whatever the reason, we all seem to identify with getting to the water.

I drove through downtown Bamberg, heading North on Highway 301. My first stop was what we locals call *"Bobcat Landing."* Not really much to see, and really just a boat landing, but it is the closest landing to downtown Bamberg. Someone probably saw a bobcat near the landing sometime back in history, and hence the name *"Bobcat Landing."*

As I pulled up to the landing, I felt relieved that no one was there and I had the landing all to myself. At first I sat in my car, but then felt the urge to get out and walk along the banks. That same soft breeze I felt at my home was also blowing through the trees along the Edisto River, making soft, smooth ripples across the water.

I began walking along the banks of the Edisto, pondering how the river was first named by the Native Americans who lived beside it, being one of the longest free flowing black water rivers in the United States. *"That is pretty impressive,* I thought. The Edisto Indians were also once originally known as the Natchez Kusso (Nah-chez Koo-so), who were a mixture of tribes, and who first lived among the Cherokee. I remembered that in the mid-1700's, the Natchez moved to Kusso lands near the Edisto river here in South Carolina. In the 1970's, the Natchez Kusso Tribe took the name *"Edisto"* in honor of the river and their ancestors.

I remembered some historic document which said that the name *"Edisto"* meant black. I also thought about what makes this river black-the decaying leaves, roots, and branches from the trees dropping into the water, and just like tea brewing, eventually the leaves let out their tannins, and the water is colored almost black. It also came to my mind that the Native Americans once called the Edisto *"Pon-Pon,"* although *"Pon Pon"* was the name supposedly given to the last 20 miles of the Edisto river before it arrives at Edisto Island, on the coast of SC. As I casually strolled along the banks, I was busy pondering some of the history of the Edisto River, at least the parts that I could remember. Much of the river's history seemed to be buried in the murky black waters of the river itself, but there if you wished to know and inquire.

Suddenly, I saw a movement directly across the river, and so I quickly stopped. All at once it was as if time changed. It was just something in the breeze, and then the light all around seemed to slightly dim, as if the sun had gone behind a cloud. I stopped for a moment, still gazing across the river at the green swaying trees, only this time I saw a very strange sight.

At first I saw a strange reflection in the water, and I then brought my eyes upward to where I saw a Native American male in full native dress, on the opposite side of the Edisto from where I was standing. He was looking regally out at the river. *"Could I actually be seeing this?"* I wondered. My senses told me that it was real, but my mind kept saying that it was just my imagination. Still, I kept on looking, wondering what more I might see. Maybe I had been reading too much about the Native Americans lately, I pondered. Also my son had found so many new artifacts-seven perfect arrowheads in one day's time! Because of this, I had artifacts and Native Americans on my mind, and perhaps that was why I saw this apparition, I mused to myself.

The Native American male saw me, but he quickly darted back underneath the low overhanging tree limbs and brush. At first I could barely hear him, but I could tell that he was running through the trees, and suddenly my hearing quickened as I followed his direction through the trees. Knowing that Native Americans usually make no sound, I knew that my hearing had somehow been quickened supernaturally. Unexpectedly, I then saw his canoe dart quickly out of the side brush, as he shoved out into the river. I stood watching as he began paddling down the sun dappled sparkling dark waters of the Edisto, and I watched until he went around the bend in the river, until I could see him no more.

I shook my head quickly, as if to shake out the cobwebs, wondering what I had just seen. *"Was it a vision, or just exactly what was it? This is the year 2017, and I should not have been seeing anything like this, right?"* I had better not tell anyone about this, I told myself.

Getting back into my car, I sat for a few minutes, thinking upon what I had just seen. Boy, this really would make someone think I had lost my marbles! Had I been reading too much about history and the Native Americans lately? Oh well, I thought, maybe it was just my imagination.

After pondering all of these things, I drove off in my little red car, heading back into Bamberg, SC, making a left onto the old Charleston-Augusta highway, which runs directly in front of Paw-Paw Country Club and golf course, in Bamberg, SC. I was intrigued by the old buffalo trail that is now a paved highway that runs just north of Bamberg SC, which I was now on.

From my study of local history, and the research of South Carolina State Historian, A.S. Salley, in *"A Narrative of Early Carolinians,"* I read that the old Charleston-Augusta Highway used to be a stagecoach route, which passed about one mile north of where Heritage Hwy (formerly highway 78) now runs, in Bamberg. I also read that most of our roads here in SC, and many other states, were once old buffalo trails. So, I was intending to ride down the *"old buffalo trail/stagecoach road"* as far as I could run it, as I made that left onto the Charleston-Augusta Highway, turning left from Highway 301.

I had driven a pretty good way down the old buffalo trail road, when suddenly I saw a flash streak across the road. It looked almost like a deer, but I knew it was a man. Whoever it was, they were moving as fast as lightning it seemed, and they were wearing buckskin. I looked quickly over to the opposite side of the road where they had run into the underbrush. Oh my, it was the same Native American man I had seen at Bobcat Landing, not fifteen minutes before! I screeched on my brakes quickly! *"Was I really seeing this or what is happening to me?"* I thought.

Much to my amazement, the Native American male did not run away this time. He just stood looking directly at me, standing proudly, as he gestured for me to follow him. I could not believe my eyes! *"Is he beckoning me to follow him, for real?"* I thought to myself. I was afraid to get out of my car, so I looked at him as I drove slowly away. *"Am I going crazy?* My God, no one would believe me, I thought again to myself. I knew I had better stop that day dreaming and get on with the task before me- driving down the old buffalo trail.

I proceeded on with my drive, trying to ignore what I had seen, and just chocking it all up to my imagination, which must have gone into overdrive, it seemed. I continued on with my drive, finally coming to stop at Hwy. 78 *(Heritage Highway)* at the crossroads of what is known as Midway. Midway was once a bustling little town, due to it being a railroad stop, which was considered about the *"midway"* point between Charleston and Hamburg, near North Augusta, SC. Passengers could get off of the train to rest, eat, and shop before the train departed once again to North-Augusta.

Time had done no justice to the once bustling little town of Midway. In fact, it is now just a small community with a crossroads, and up until recently, one small store. I tried to imagine what Midway must have once been like in my mind's eye. As time goes by, many towns disappear, and for whatever reasons, other towns come up nearby, which outgrow and surpass the others. Such is the present day Midway, it's hey day gone by, with only a crossroads as a reminder of the past. The town of Bamberg, SC seems to have bypassed the small town of Midway by leaps and bounds.

Also, there is evidence that the Edisto tribe of the Muskogian Indians once lived and hunted around the area known as Bamberg. Early settlers then arrived, following the Native Americans. Some of the earliest white settlers were German, Swiss, Scots-Irish, English, and Huguenots (of Orangeburg, SC) who moved south across both forks of the Edisto River, settling in present day Bamberg county. My history did indeed seem to be coming back to me.

But, back to my drive along the old buffalo trail. I had in mind to go straight across at the crossroads there at Midway, which continues the old buffalo trail/stagecoach road, but I felt the strange urge to turn left onto hwy. 78 heading toward Branchville and Charleston, SC. I could always come back and drive along the rest of the buffalo trail when I came back through later, I thought.

Continuing my drive along highway 78 toward Branchville, SC, I suddenly had another strange urge to turn down a dirt road to the left, a few miles out. As I turned down this small dirt road, not even knowing where I was going, it was as if I was being drawn by some unknown force. I had in mind to turn around if the road became too grown over. *"Why in the world am I going down this unknown dirt road?"* I wondered to myself. Still I knew that this unknown *"force"* was urging me to continue on.

What was happening to me then reminded me of the time that I was in a library, looking for something to read, when a big book simply fell off of the shelf right in front of me. Of course, I checked the book out; it was an account of Native American history, which I never forgot. It seems that all of my life I have had these strange type of occurrences happen to me, as if I was being directed as to which way to go. Also, I knew by now to take heed of that direction.

Following that strange *"urge"* to go down that obscure dirt road, I noticed the brush was getting thicker and thicker and the road began going seemingly downhill. I finally came to some very narrow ruts in the road, which still had some water in them. I was afraid to drive through those muddy ruts, and I had in mind to begin backing up. I felt that I had gone about as far as I could go on this adventure.

That is when I again saw the same Native American man, standing directly in front of my car this time. It was as if he appeared out of nowhere, it seemed. He made motions with his hands, as if telling me to back up into a certain area of overgrown brush. Something just told me to do it, and I did. To my surprise, I backed onto a very firm area of dirt, which would enable me to turn my car around and then leave the same way I drove in. I was shocked and surprised at my own self for actually *"listening"* to this Native American, who could simply be nothing but a figment of my own imagination, I feared.

"Ok, now I can speed away from whatever this apparition is that has been following me along my drive," I thought. Yet, just as I was about to speed away, this man or apparition, as I was not sure which, motioned for me to open my door, and I actually listened to him, even knowing he was a stranger. Still, I wondered in my mind, *"How can this be real?"* If this was a dream, it was quickly turning into a very strange adventure, I thought. *"If I am asleep and dreaming, then Dear Lord, please wake me up,"* I pleaded.

Much to my surprise, this Native American began talking to me in English, although a strange sounding English. It almost sounded like King James English to me, which I was familiar with from reading my 1611 King James English Bible. He was using *"thees"* and *"thous"* just like my King James Bible. OK, now that is really strange, I thought, a Native American speaking something like King James English? This was not making sense to me at all.

He told me that I did not have to be afraid of him, and that he was there to take me on a journey along the Edisto River. He managed to convey to me that our final destination was to visit his Indian village, after first visiting his friends who were white English people. He explained to me that his white friends had taught him of the white man's English God, and how to read.

Now, I knew that there was a reason I was here with this Native American, and that there was something I was supposed to learn from him. So, I asked him why was he here to take me to see all of these things-why me-of all people? He then told me that I was there to find out about my Native American ancestors, as well as my white ancestors. He also told me that the answers I had sought throughout the years were in the dreams I had been given, and would be revealed by the end of our journey.

Well, as intriguing as this sounded to me, I was still very reluctant to go on this journey, as I was not sure if this was real, a delusion or perhaps even an open eyed daydream. Even more so, could he be some sort of time traveler? Yet, something in me wanted to go so badly, and I knew that I could learn much from this man. I also sensed no danger in him, and he was very polite. I was also very curious about his white English friends, and how they had taught him about the white man's God. Most of all, I could tell that he had a good and friendly spirit. He did not look like some Native American wanting to harm me, like those stereotypical accounts of savage Indians that I later came to learn, have been falsely promoted by Hollywood movies. I could sense that he was peaceful, and I was pleased at that. So, trusting my gut reaction to this man, I felt safe with him immediately. I also agreed to leave my car there, hidden in the underbrush, and off I went with this Native American man, walking behind him, as he led me down the little dirt road, which ended at the Edisto River.

He told me that we would be traveling by canoe. I assumed that it was the same canoe he had shoved out into the river at Bobcat Landing, near Bamberg, when I had first caught a glimpse of him. I also noticed that the canoe was not what I had pictured a regular Native American canoe to be. The canoe he had was what is known as a *"dugout"* canoe, since it had been carved or dug out of a single tree. I only thought of canoes as being made of birch bark, learned by seeing the small souvenir copies that tourists buy. *"How fascinating,"* I thought, as he helped me into the canoe, gesturing for me to sit down in the front. I got into the front and he sat in the back, just as he had indicated for me to do.

Soon we were out into the Edisto River, the Native American steering the canoe along peacefully. As I turned to look back at the landing, I noticed his long black hair shining in the sun. *"Oh my,"* I thought for perhaps the hundredth time, *"is this real? Am I really floating down the Edisto River with a Native American Indian who speaks the King's English?"*

I quickly forgot my hesitation however, as we progressed along our journey down the river. I couldn't help but gaze at the familiar serene forests of yellow pine, oak, and the many cypress trees with overhanging moss, which I had known and loved, walking in and among them most of my life.

I had always loved the familiar smell of pine and cedar especially. The smell brought back memories of my teenage years, when I used to take my guitar down into the piney woods near my old home place, where I would play and sing songs to the Lord. Yes, these trees were my old friends, ones I had not seen or appreciated in such a long time. Those trees, or those similar to them, were my audience as I had praised God in the serenity of the pine forest near my childhood home. Once more inhaling the natural perfumed aroma of the pine, oak, and cypress, I soaked in all that I was seeing.

The many different trees went quickly by in my immediate vision, almost in a blur it seemed. The sound of the Native American steering the canoe seemed to be the only sound I heard, except for the call of the wild birds, and other chirping creatures. An otter scurried quickly into the water from one of the opposite banks of the river, surprising me, but I was more concerned about where I was being taken by this unknown Native American man. It was still uncanny that I now had absolutely no fear of this man, but that was a good thing. My heart had been put to rest when I had first gazed into his eyes. Some say the *"soul"* shows through the eyes, and all I can say is that the look in his eyes was full of peace and love.

As we continued to progress along the river, I began to notice that things seemed somehow different; something in the atmosphere had changed. As we rounded a particular bend in the river, I then saw the most incredible sight. How it could be possible, I didn't know. We actually passed through a rainbow, which was stretched out over the river like an arch. It was like passing through an entrance to another world.

Immediately after we passed beneath that rainbow, paddling on down the river, I heard the howling of a wolf in the woods. It gave me shivers at first, but my Native American escort pointed in a particular direction on the banks of the Edisto, and I then saw a big white wolf. My Native American guide then began pulling our canoe over to the banks of the river. All of my own instincts went wild then, because surely this man wasn't pulling us over to the banks of the river, with a wild wolf howling and tracking us along the banks? Yet, that was just what he was doing.

I was more than uneasy as he pulled us over to the banks of the river, got out and pulled the canoe ashore. He then motioned for me to step out of the canoe also. Being petrified with fear of the wolf, I shook my head, crossing my arms, implying a very big NO! He once again motioned, and I again obstinately shook my head NO! Then, the most incredible thing happened. My Native American guide cupped his hands together and made a strange sound, and out of the woods ran this big white wolf; yes, the one we had just heard howling in the woods. The big white wolf then ran up to my Native American guide, looking from him to me. I was very aware that the Native American was talking to the white wolf in his native language, and it appeared that the white wolf was actually listening. From that moment on, I began to refer to this white wolf as *"White Wolf."*

I saw then that *"White Wolf"* had great intelligence and seemed almost like a person. My Native American guide then proceeded to tell me to talk to the wolf, and that I must ask its permission to go farther on this journey, because we were in its territory. *"Say WHAT?"* I loudly exclaimed! *"Yeah right, I am really going to speak English to a wolf and he is going to UNDERSTAND me?"* My Native American guide then most adamantly told me that he would take me back if I did not ask permission of the wolf.

OK, so there I was with a very real dilemma. I had to pretend to talk to the white wolf, or either I would be taken back. That wasn't much of a choice, I thought to myself. I finally decided to go along with it all, but I was not feeling too good about any of it. Yeah right, talking wolves! Yet, I knew I had to do it or be banished from this most wonderful unknown world. However, something pricked the back of my mind, and I then remembered a piece of a story that I had read in some extra-Biblical book, about how it was once believed that the animals in the Garden of Eden could talk. According to that book, the animals had lost their ability to speak after the serpent (devil) spoke to Eve and tempted her, and thus caused the whole fall of man. However, I knew that animals in our day and time just did NOT talk back to us.

So, with my Native American guide looking on, I slowly but hesitantly spoke to the *"White Wolf."*

The white wolf had the bluest eyes you had ever seen, almost like an Alaskan husky, and they seemed to glow as he looked at me. I knew beyond the shadow of a doubt that this was NO ordinary wolf.

"I, I, I ask your permission to journey through your territory," I stammered half heartedly to the white wolf. To my surprise, the wolf began speaking back to me in English and I could suddenly understand him. He told me not to be afraid of the journey, but to open myself up to all that I must learn from it. He also said that he would be following us the whole way, as our guardian. He said that we might not see him at times, but to always know that he was there, and would protect us and show us the way, if need be.

Oh my, I had so many questions to ask this White Wolf, now that I could understand him. Then my Native American escort spoke to the wolf, and I could suddenly hear and understand their whole conversation, almost like two people speaking to each other in English in front of me. My hearing had somehow been miraculously opened up to understand them both, I guess. I then joined in the conversation with them both, asking more questions which the wolf quickly answered.

The *"White Wolf"* looked directly at me again, and said that he wanted me to meet his family. *"What?"* I thought, with even more incredulity! *"Did this speaking white wolf just say that he wanted me to meet his FAMILY?"* Did I hear correctly, I thought, or was I in some very vivid wild dream with talking animals? After all, my mind was still struggling to understand all that was happening to me.

My Native American guide told me that we were indeed going to journey and meet the White Wolf's family. Again, I told him to go on without me. Again, like before, he insisted very adamantly that I must go with them, because it was the wish and will of the white wolf, and that it was a great honor to be asked to meet his family. The Native American gave me a look that said if I didn't do as I was asked, that he might just force me to go along with them anyway. And so, I reluctantly got out of the safety of the dug out canoe and went with them onto a narrow path into the deep woods, the White Wolf guarding us all the while, or so it appeared to me.

All three of us traversed the narrow path for a ways, when I spotted another grown white wolf and three smaller baby white wolves, hidden in the bushes. The big *"White Wolf"* that we had just *"met"* went over to what I presumed to be his *"family"* and nuzzled the grown white wolf, who must have been his mate. She then drew the three baby white wolves nearer to her. The big *"White Wolf"* then turned around, standing proudly in front of his *"family"* and told me that this was his wife and children. I nodded my head and said that I was glad to meet them. The *"wife"* wolf nodded her head up and down but did not speak, as only the male white wolf had spoken.

Immediately after the female nodded her head, I had a sudden flash or memory of seeing the *"White Wolf"* and his family in one of my dreams from the past, but try as I might, I could only remember a flash of it. In my heart, I then felt something let go, and it felt like I was being infused with a shot of pure love, and not a sensual earthly love either, but a divine love. My heart seemed as if it would overflow with a heavenly supernatural love! After that feeling of incredible love, the most incredible peace permeated my soul, and I knew that I then had *"permission"* to proceed on with this journey.

My Native American guide and I then proceeded to make our way back to the canoe, the white male wolf following behind us this time, instead of in front of us. We arrived back at the dug out canoe, and I was mighty glad to see that canoe, as it meant safety to me. He motioned for me to get into the front of the canoe, and he then got into the back. We then shoved off from the banks of the Edisto, the male white wolf watching us all the while with those glowing icy blue eyes. I knew that I would not ever forget the things he said, and later on I would come to understand more of what the white wolf meant. He was the *"guardian"* to the entrance of this spiritual dream world that I had entered, if this was indeed a dream. I had much to learn, but had no idea at the time just exactly how much.

We continued on, making our way down the black waters of the Edisto, its black water shining in the dappled sunlight like jewels on the water. I had much to think about, and pondered all that I had seen so far. While we were paddling along, I spotted a flock of wild turkeys on the banks of the river, but they were all of incredible size-each one must have weighed over forty pounds! I had never seen wild turkeys that large, and knew that it was very rare to come upon a wild turkey of that size.

"Incredible," I thought, *"I had seen a whole flock of wild turkeys that were larger than any I had ever seen."* As we continued on down the river, I also saw what looked like a sort of wild parakeet. *"A parakeet, here in the woods in South Carolina?"* I thought. I could not believe what I was seeing. I was seeing more wildlife at one time than I had ever seen on the Edisto.

In the river I also saw fish of the most incredible size, jumping straight up out of the water; bass, trout, brim. It was almost as if they were trying to jump into the canoe. They too were larger than any normal fish I had seen in my modern day and time, just as the wild turkeys were larger than normal. *"What is happening here?"* I wondered. Many coveys of very huge quail flew and scurried on the sides of the banks of the river, and five or six raccoons ran down to the water's edge, picking up clams with their little paws, not even running away when they saw us. I was truly amazed as I saw such an incredible increase in wildlife all around. There was absolutely no doubt about it, they were literally coming out of the *"wood"* work.

A whole family of deer stood on one of the opposing banks as we drifted by, just staring leisurely at us, not running away at all. I was very puzzled, and knew that something strange had happened, although I could not fathom exactly what it was. Why were all of these animals coming forth along the banks, and why weren't they afraid of us? They appeared to have no fear of man at all. I suddenly remembered that everything must have changed when we had passed under that rainbow that had seemed to drape itself over the river like an arch. The rainbow must have been a portal to this strange world that I was in now, a world that must be back in time, when the white settlers had first come to settle the Americas.

Suddenly, the Native American rowed the canoe to the banks of the river, after we had been on the river for what seemed like an hour. He motioned for me to stay in the canoe, however, and so I did. He walked silently off in Indian style, never making a sound. I looked deep into the woods, shading my eyes, and saw what looked like a wild panther dash across the path the Indian had taken. *"I hope he comes back soon,"* I thought, as fear again began creeping into my mind.

Sure enough, and just in time to qualm my fears, my Native American guide came back with a stack of deerskin hides, all rolled up together and tied with leather strapping. He then carefully placed them in the bottom of the canoe. *"Hmmm,"* I wondered, *"what is he going to do with all of those hides?"* I finally worked up the courage to ask him bluntly, *"Where are we going?"* He answered me, saying simply, *"We go to the Branch."* The Branch? I wondered what he could possibly have meant by that. Once again, my gut told me not to ask this man too many questions at that point in time, so I remained silent when he did not answer back.

After approximately thirty minutes of paddling down the Edisto, he pulled to the banks once again.

This time he motioned for me to get out of the canoe, as he pulled the canoe up onto the banks, placing small limbs and brush over it to camouflage it, I supposed. He then motioned for me to follow him. I didn't want to be left alone, and so I got out of the canoe and followed after him. I looked and saw a small path in front of us that led into the deep piney forest. He motioned to it, saying once again, *"We go to the Branch."*

As we trekked through the woods on the way to *"The Branch,"* as he had called it, I began to wonder about all of the wild animals I had seen along the banks, and the prolific wildlife that I had never seen or even heard of on the Edisto. I knew that this was not the Edisto of today, but that I was most assuredly now seeing the Edisto in a former state in time. From my historic reading, I vaguely remembered back when South Carolina was first settled, and how there were reports that had to be made back to England, on the status of the land- was it good for settling? I remembered a description of the land, described as very fertile; that description seeming an awful lot like what I had just seen on my journey down the Edisto river.

Thinking back, it appeared as if the entire landscape had changed when we came to that certain bend in the river where we had paddled underneath that rainbow that was stretched across the river. All I knew is that I wanted to see more of this strange land that surrounded the Edisto river- an Edisto that I had never seen before, or even imagined could exist. I wanted to see more of this land along the river that was plentiful in some of the largest wild game I had ever seen, and trees that were larger and taller than any trees I had ever gazed upon. Whatever this journey was, I wanted to know and see more.

All of a sudden, I and my native friend entered a small grassy meadow sheltered among the huge pine trees. Standing stately and proud, he pointed for me to look and see. What looked like thousands of yellow/gold colored butterflies were flitting and dancing in the dappled sunlight that was bouncing off of their wings. It looked like myriads of stars dancing on the water, except it was the sunlight glancing off of their wings. As if I were in some trance, I stood perfectly still, awed at seeing these beautiful butterflies. My native friend then managed to awaken me from that strange hypnotic butterfly trance, just in time to motion for me to look up high above the flitting butterflies to see a majestic eagle in flight. *"What an amazing sight to see,"* I thought to myself. It looked almost as if this great eagle was flying in slow motion, as he descended from the lofty heights and began a descent. Inside my heart, I knew that this great eagle was coming straight to us, and amazingly, I had no fear.

At that moment, after looking up at the eagle, my Native American guide held out his hand in anticipation of the great eagle landing there. I noticed that he had wrapped a piece of hide on his forearm, and the great majestic eagle then came and landed there, much like a carrier pigeon would do to its master. Then, just as my native friend had spoken his own native language to the "*White Wolf*", he again spoke this same native language to what I called, "The Great Eagle." Just as with the

"White Wolf," I could not understand their native language, but I was certainly getting used to animals that talked.

After my native friend and this "Great Eagle" conversed, the eagle then turned his eyes to me, and began to speak. *"We have met before you and I,"* he said to me. Inside I felt as if it was the truth, and so I began trying to remember....and suddenly I remembered seeing this "Great Eagle" before!

"Yes, I do remember you," I replied. *"You got my attention one day when I was driving in my car to Orangeburg, SC, and there you were, a rare bald eagle just SITTING on the ground by the side of the road, staring at me as I drove by,"* I said to him.

Again the "Great Eagle" spoke to me, *"Yes, I watched for you as you drove by on the road. I was waiting there for you."* Replying back to him, I said, *"I thought something strange that day when I saw you, and I felt as if something awakened in me then, but I could not put my finger on just what it was."* Continuing on talking to the "Great Eagle," I said, *"When I looked at you just sitting there on the side of the road, it was almost as if you were human, and not a bird. Also, after I saw you that day, I began having many more dreams and visions than I had ever had in my entire life, and they have not let up even to this day."*

After I said this, the "Great Eagle" seemed to suddenly have a soft glimmer in his eye. Then the "Great Eagle" said something very important, *"A higher vision was awakened in you that day, and the more you follow the spirit inside of you, the* more you will understand your own destiny in this life. The dreams and visions are showing you the way, and they are gifts from God. But I cannot tell you anymore at this time. This is also why you are on this journey, you and many others like you." Then the "Great Eagle" lifted off from my native friends hand and flew majestically back into the sky.

As the "Great Eagle" disappeared from our sight, my native friend then told me to look at the ground just in front of my feet. Not knowing why, I did as he said, and saw a tip of flint sticking up out of the dirt. He motioned for me to dig it up, and so I bent down and began to dig the piece of flint up from out of the earth. Up from that rich, fertile dirt came the most beautiful perfect arrowhead, and I brushed it off carefully.

While brushing the dirt carefully off of the arrowhead, I looked at my native friend, as if to say, can I keep it? He nodded his head yes, motioning that it was a *"gift"* to me from the "Great Eagle." Wanting to get back on our journey, he also patted his side as if to tell me to put it in the pocket of my blue jeans. I carefully put it in my right pocket and we continued on.

What an awesome gift that was for me, but I had to wonder still if all this was a dream, or a delusion, and would I still have that arrowhead when it was all over? Of course I wouldn't, especially if this was a dream, I thought to myself. Only time will tell, I mused.

My native friend then asked me a very important question, *"When the "Great Eagle" told you to continue to follow the spirit that is inside you, what did that mean to you?"* I then replied to him, *"At first I thought that would conflict with my beliefs in God and Jesus Christ, because I am a Christian, but then I realized that he was referring to the Holy Spirit inside of me."* *"Yes, that is right,"* said my native friend. *"Many people of today's time believe that the Native Americans were nothing but savages. That falsehood was taught in all of the school books of long ago and even today. America, as you know it, has a false image of the spirituality of the true Native American."*

As my Native American guide spoke these words to me, I knew deep inside that what he had said was true, and I began to feel a terrible sadness. Tears welled up in my eyes for no reason, it seemed to me. Yet, I knew these tears were for the people I had somehow unknowingly looked down upon. I knew then that I had also believed that same propaganda that was taught to me. I had watched the many westerns on TV that had shown Hollywood actors falsely portraying Native Americans as nothing but savages scalping white people.

I began sensing that this was going to be a big part of the destiny of my journey back in time, to learn the truth about my ancestors. As the "Great Eagle" had confirmed to me, my vision was to rise much higher, and he was a sign and confirmation of that. Thinking back, I had first seen the Great Eagle about eight years before, and as things began lining up in my mind, I realized that my inner vision had steadily been progressing since that day.

You see, eagles fly ever so much higher than the other birds. They are said to have *"an eagle eye"* since eagles can spot their prey from miles away. They fly higher and can see better than the other birds.

At the same time, I also remembered that as a little eight year old girl, while falling asleep every night, I felt as if I was like an eagle, with great wings spread. I would take that nightly flight, flying and soaring over beautiful golden fields of grain. Then the dream would turn into a nightmare every night, when after miles of soaring like an eagle, I would begin descending to the ground, right over a pit with many writhing snakes trying to cover and consume me. Each night during many years of my childhood, I would wake up crying from that same dream, as it haunted me every single night.

All at once, I suddenly knew the meaning of the "Great Eagle!" I had soared like an eagle when I was young, but the snakes were obstacles from the enemy of my soul which later appeared in my life, trying to crush and break my spirit, which for a time they did.

I had struggled long and hard in my life, but eventually found the Lord Jesus Christ. Finding Jesus helped me to be able to rise up once again and soar on the wings of eagles, and to run and not be weary, and to walk and not faint!

The Bible verse I needed suddenly came back to me, just when I needed it the most:

Isaiah 40:31:

"But they that wait upon the LORD shall renew their strength; they shall mount up with wings as eagles; they shall run , and not be weary ; and they shall walk , and not faint. "

Yes, I suddenly realized that it was after I had found the Lord that the "Great Eagle" appeared to me on the side of the road, looking into my soul with those piercing eagle eyes, eight years before. And now, the "Great Eagle" had appeared to me once again, while on this journey.

I also knew then, more than at any other time, that this was a very special journey back in time. I also knew that I was finally on the right path, at just the right time. I was right in the middle of my destiny, canoeing down the Edisto River of long ago with my Native American *"guide,"* the *"White Wolf"* as my *"Guardian,"* and the higher vision of the *"Great Eagle"* to show things to me that I had never before seen. I knew at that moment, that I would no longer remain sitting on the ground, like the *"Great Eagle"* who had first appeared to me, but that I was going to soar and fly, which was my destiny.

CHAPTER 2: THE BRANCH

Progressing on toward *"The Branch,"* as my Native American guide called it, we then passed through many meadows, swampy areas, and huge fields of pine trees. I also saw even more herds of deer everywhere all around us grazing, and just like the other wildlife I had seen earlier, they didn't run like the deer we see today.

I also saw such beautiful wildflowers everywhere, and I marveled at their astounding, unearthly surreal beauty, as they swayed in the breeze. I had never seen wildflowers with such amazing colors! To my amazement, I even saw peach, and several fig trees. I just could not get over the abundant beauty of this land that I was seeing; whether by dream, vision, or reality, at that point I did not care which.

As my native friend and I traveled on deeper into the woods, it became evident to me that this must be a well traveled Indian footpath. I was continually amazed, just as before, as I saw wild grape vines laden with the most delectable bunches of grapes, hanging all along the sides of the path, not very far off and easy to reach. I motioned to my friend that I wanted to pick a bunch of those grapes that were growing everywhere, as I was by then getting a little hungry.

He allowed us to stop for a moment, and I picked a bunch of the very large wild grapes, popping a few of them into my mouth. They were the most delectable grapes I had ever tasted! I had most assuredly never seen wild grapes growing like that in the woods anywhere around here.

My hunger satiated, we walked on, getting ever closer to our destination, which was still unknown to me. I looked at the ground beneath my feet as we were walking steadily to our destination called *"The Branch."* I noticed that the dirt was also very different than the usual dirt I had seen anywhere around this area, in my own time. I stooped over and scooped up a handful of this rich, black, dark dirt, and I could see that it was truly a more fertile type of dirt than I had ever seen before. My native friend looked at me strangely, but then motioned for us to continue on.

"No wonder the wild grapes were growing so abundantly and had plentiful bunches of grapes on them." I thought. It was all because of the rich, fertile dirt, yet untouched by white man or plow. Oh

how this saddened me, knowing that in my modern world of 2017, the land had been basically "raped" and stripped of a lot of the minerals and nutrients that made its bounty so healthy to eat. People in today's time have to buy "organic" to try and make sure they got produce grown from good soil, but the soil could not really ever be the same as I was seeing it then. I was actually seeing what true ORGANIC meant, as I gazed at that rich soil of yesteryear.

My Native American guide told me, as I was staring at that dark fertile soil, that once a man could accidentally drop a seed from his pocket, and a plant would grow anywhere. The land was just that fertile back then.

My native guide also told me to look long and hard at those grapes, because, just as I had been musing, the grapes and fruits of today had all been corrupted. He explained that the white man had put unnatural chemicals and pesticides into the land and onto the fruit and vegetables themselves, poisoning not only the land, but also the people who ate the fruit of the vine and of the land. Native American's did not pollute the land. The land, or "Mother Earth," was sacred to them. While gazing at that fertile soil, a deep sorrow kept growing inside me.

I began to get curious about what was happening to me, and finally decided to work up the courage to ask my Native American friend what his name was. He paused for a moment, and then said *"Shantoo." "Shantoo? What kind of name is that,"* I wondered to myself. He's probably making that up anyway, I thought. But then, I remembered that Native Americans don't speak with deception about themselves in the way everyone in the white man's world seems to do today. So, I was being taken on a journey by a Native American named Shantoo! I finally had a name for my native friend.

I also began pondering once more on the many different varieties of trees, more so than was normal. As we walked on through the woods, I saw red cedar, birch, ash, and even a walnut tree. All of the trees were very large, much larger than normal. The pines were also taller and larger than any I had seen before, standing from 60 to 80 feet tall, as I had first seen before now. In fact, the oaks themselves were huge and there were so many big oaks to behold everywhere. I knew then that I was truly seeing the country surrounding the Edisto River the way that it must have been when the Edisto Indians lived there long ago. This realization never ceased to amaze me.

I really began putting two and two together then. If my Native American guide Shantoo was speaking a form of King James English to me, with *"thees"* and *"thous,"* then the time period must have been somewhere in the early 1600's, based on what I could remember from my study of history. I reasoned that if I had been transported back in time, or if this was even a dream, I was surely seeing this land in its pristine, unpolluted state. I did not want to miss a moment of it, either, dream, vision or not. The question kept bothering me, however; why was this Native American speaking King James English to me? That was a mystery that

I hoped would be solved somewhere during this journey.

Farther along on the Indian path, Shantoo motioned for me to follow close behind him. He stopped just under a tree, and pointed for me to look up. I jumped back as I saw a mountain lion reclining on a tree limb just above us. The mountain lion had been resting on the limb of that tree, and we had disturbed him in our passing through, but he just quietly watched us as we passed on by. Thank goodness the mountain lion did not make a move to pounce, or I would have been more frightened than what I already was. The presence of Shantoo reassured me that there was no danger, however. I also had the sense about me to know that having a Native American guide escorting me was about as good as it could get in this wild country, unknown to me, but so familiar to Shantoo.

As we kept walking, I asked Shantoo about the tall trees, and I commented on how they were so much taller than in my day and time. He told me that the dirt I had held in my hand was so much more fertile back then, but that now the white man had come and stripped the land of its nutrients that made the soil so rich. I had already guessed that, but I wanted to hear it from him.

Shantoo also explained that when the white man had first come (in the time we had gone back to) they had wanted room to plant gardens, and needed logs for homes. Without any thought, the white man began cutting down trees for all of this. Shantoo explained that the white man had looked down on the Native Americans because they did not *"clear the land"* of the trees, but planted their *"maize"* or corn where there was a natural clearing, so as not to cut down the trees.

In effect, the white man thought they were smarter than the Native American's because the natives did not cut down the trees and make spots for gardens. What the white man did not realize, explained Shantoo, is that the Native American had respect for all of God's creation, including trees. Shantoo explained to me then how his people believed that they were *"stewards"* or keepers of God's creation, the earth. They believed that all life here on earth had been created by God and that it was sacred, and not to be destroyed unless it was for food or necessity. He explained that this was why Native American's refer to earth as *"Mother Earth,"* he explained. Mother Earth sustained them. Mother Earth's nutrients were what made the crops and trees and vegetation grow, and we needed those nutrients for our bodies to live.

Ah yes, I was now beginning to get a much better understanding of why the white man who first came to America to settle, thought they were so superior to the Native Americans. Also, Shantoo explained that a Native American was true to their word. When they gave their word, they did not break it. Then the white man came along and his people believed that the white man also kept their word. They later found out the hard way, that the white man made treaties and vows to the Native Americans that they did not keep, and cheated them.

That was why when the whites smoked the peace pipes with the Native Americans, the natives believed the smoke went up to God as a sacred witness, and so they would have never dreamed it did not mean the same to a white man, or that one could lie. Yet, the white man smoked the pipe with them and did lie. What was sacred to the Native American, was not sacred to the whites.

My understanding was being enlightened as to what had really happened back then. The white man for some reason had not learned about honor and keeping their word, although there were some whites who did keep their word, Shantoo explained. However, those few whites who honored the Native Americans were few and far between, according to Shantoo.

"If the white man had kept his word, and had not come to overtake the land, but live here in peace with the Native Americans, all of this tragedy would not have happened," Shantoo said, and then abruptly stopped speaking, gazing straight ahead as if he was in another world. I knew not to press him for answers anymore at that time. I had truly been given much to think upon by my Native American friend.

As we continued on with our walk, Shantoo kept the roll of deerskin hides on his back. He shifted the hides and then stopped for a moment, checking them and readjusting the roll. He then pointed ahead on the path. I could then see a line of smoke rising up through the pine and oak trees. *"The Branch"* he said as he pointed to the smoke.

We traveled on as a clearing appeared up ahead, dotted with a gathering of many people. I saw many Native Americans and many white men, as well. The "Branch" appeared to be a small trading post or camp. Before we got to the main area of what appeared to be this large gathering of Indians and white men waiting to sell hides or to trade, I noticed an unusually large oak tree, much larger than any I had seen in the woods on the way to this camp. This particular oak was very huge, and it seemed that the traders and Indians must surely have used this large oak as a landmark.

Shantoo motioned for me to come over to the big oak. As I got close to the big oak, he pointed to two branches on the monstrous sized tree, informing me that one branch pointed the way towards what is Orangeburg SC today, and the other pointed westerly towards what is now Bamberg, SC.

"The Branch," he said again, pointing to first one branch of the tree, and then the other. Finally, I got it! This place was called *"The Branch"* because the two branches of the huge oak were at the meeting point where two Indian footpaths converged. That was an ah ha moment, and I shook my head up and down to let him know I then understood just what *"The Branch"* meant. Yes, we had arrived at *"The Branch!"*

I realized then that we must have walked through the woods on a smaller Indian footpath, all the way to what is today known as Branchville, SC, from the Edisto River near Bamberg, SC, hiking through the woods. I also noticed that the two main Indian footpaths to which the branches of the huge oak tree pointed, were much larger footpaths.

Standing directly under the old oak, sure enough, one of its big branches pointed directly west, to the Indian trail going westward out of this *"camp"* toward Bamberg, SC. The Indian footpath would have eventually ended up at what was once called old *"Fort Monroe,"* an Indian Trading Post, now the town of North Augusta, SC. I walked over to the other *"branch"* of the old oak, which pointed to the north, and which followed the north Edisto River toward what is now Orangeburg, SC, and continued on to the old town of Granby, now known as Cayce, SC.

Standing under that old oak, Shantoo began to explain to me how white men referred to most Native Americans as *"Indians,"* and that some folks we might meet would say *"Native Americans"* but others might say *"Indians."* I was beginning to see how much my modern day world was different from the world of the 1600's, and our journey had only just begun.

Shantoo then told the story that the Native American named Bear Heart had told: *"I don't always feel comfortable in talking about Indians; even the word "Indian" itself is very misunderstood. When Columbus found Native people here, they were gentle people who accepted him, so Columbus wrote in his journal, 'These are people of God.' In his language, he wrote "In Dios." Later the s was dropped and Indio eventually became Indian, which originated as "people of God." -The wind is my mother, Bear Heart.:"* What a story that was, that the Native Americans became known as *"Indians"* simply because Columbus called them "In Dios" which actually meant people of God, and all because someone had dropped the s.

Shantoo then turned and glanced around him at the trading post. As I also looked around this place called *"The Branch,"* I saw horses laden down with hides tied to them. *"Hmm,"* I wondered. I was curious about horses being around during this time frame. Being perplexed, I tried as best I could to remember my history of this area, and sure enough, pieces of history began coming back to me.

Ah, ha! It was believed that Hernando De Soto might possibly have come through this area on his way to what is now known as Orangeburg, South Carolina. I also remembered that according to the historic accounts, he had come to a place that is today called *"cannons bridge."* *"Cannons Bridge"* road of today was not far from the small Indian footpath we had just traversed to get to *"The Branch."* I was slowly but surely piecing it all together.

I still could not help but ask Shantoo about the presence of the horses in camp. They had piqued my curiosity. Shantoo pointed to the horses and said, *"Sky Dogs!"* *"Horses come from captured horses of De Soto by Chickasaw indians. Chickasaw breed them with other horses, then trade to other Indians. Horses come from the first De Soto horses."*

BANKS OF THE EDISTO: A Journey In Time

Well, that explained the presence of these horses to me, who were bred from some of the original Spanish horses from Hernando De Soto. Wow, this was really pretty awesome to me, and I was busy trying to take it all in.

"You thought all Indians rode horses and raided white people didn't you? Shantoo asked. *"Yes, I did, Shantoo,"* I hated to admit. *"You must erase the image of your Hollywood Western Indian, and you must replace it with the truth you are being shown,"* Shantoo said. *"Remember that you are on this journey to find TRUTH, and I am your guide to the truth,"* said Shantoo in perfect modern day English that time.

"Those images that your Hollywood movies portrayed caused you to believe that all Indians rode bareback on horses and raided the whites. All Indians were portrayed as horsemen, but that was false. The truth is that the Indians of the Southwest region were the Indians that were mounted on horses. In another region, the Navajo, Apache and Comanche were tribes known as being " mounted," Shantoo went on to explain.

"The Comanche were actually the horse-oriented tribe that was depicted in your movies from Hollywood. The Apache, on the other hand, were actually known as very poor horsemen, and usually fought their battles on foot. The Navajo used their ponies for tending sheep and cattle because they were herdsmen. So you see, Hollywood portraying all Indians as riding horses would be like my believing that all white people wore hats, simply

because I had seen a few whites wearing hats." Shantoo explained.

Ok, I was getting this now, I truly was. Most of what I had learned about Native Americans had come from some false image made up by white men. My mind was busy absorbing all of this new knowledge, and there was truly much to absorb. I was seeing the equivalent of history coming alive, except that I was in the history book myself now.

Shantoo went on to explain how horses were introduced to the Native Americans by the white man. *"The Native Americans had done without horses for almost 20,000 years before the white man had introduced them to them,"* Shantoo continued on. That statement caused me to really stop and think. *" Well, then what did the Native American's use before they had horses?"* I couldn't help but *ask*. *"Dogs carried our supplies before horses came,"* Shantoo replied.

Everything Shantoo was telling me was so very interesting to me, and I couldn't wait to hear more. I sensed though, that Shantoo was getting very quiet, and I knew this was my que not to ask anymore questions at that time.

This was all very fascinating to me, but seeing some of the descendants of Hernando De Soto's horses excited me because I had heard so much about De Soto. I wanted to go over and look at them more closely, but knew that I could not do it at that time, since I saw Shantoo shake his head no to me. Also, he made a sign to me that seemed to imply that he would tell me more later, about these

"Sky Dogs." I was not exactly sure how I was now able to interpret his sign language, when at first I had no clue. Things really were becoming more clear to me as we journeyed on.

Also, on some of the horses I saw crude pots, pans and utensils tied to the sides along with hides, and other various items that were obviously for trade, such as guns, powder, hatchets, shot, kettles, fabric, blankets and trinkets such as beads. When I saw the beads, I could not help but feel sadness at knowing how the white man had cheated the Native Americans so much in trade and had taken advantage of their goodness and honor. Not all whites in colonial days were bad, however, and even Shantoo had admitted that, but the ones who had deceit in their hearts made it hard on those who were not that way, and so good whites and Native Americans both suffered, because of those whites who were dishonest.

Seeing those beads also brought to my mind the story about how Columbus had said the native americans were a *"people of God"* and were so humble. To cheat these *"people of God"* was a terrible crime in my eyes, as I am sure it was to God.

Continuing to look around, I noticed whole families of Indians-women and children, who had seemingly set up camp and were cooking corn cakes, cooked over the open fire. Campfires were going and the women were also busy tending to their children while cooking. Traders milled back and forth in this camp, and I was truly amazed at so much activity. I was still astounded, realizing that I was standing in the very spot of where the old town of the original Branchville, SC was located. The only difference is that I was seeing the town as it must have been in the 1600's. What a very strange feeling that was for me.

Shantoo explained to me, this time switching back to his broken English, that three different camps of Indians co-existed together there at *"The Branch."* One was called the *"Beech"* camp, another the *"Pen"* camp and the other one the *"Sunset"* camp. I noticed that the *"Sunset"* Indian camp was near the westerly side of *"The Branch,"* which was probably why it was called just that, being situated more toward the setting of the sun. I also suspected that the *"Beech"* camp might have reflected the Indians who had lived near a Beech tree. Why the other camp called themselves the Pen camp was not clear to me, and so I had no real clue, except that perhaps a white English settler named Pen must have befriended them. Still, this was just my own surmising. Yes, I could only speculate as to why these three Indian camps were called by those names.

Everyone seemed to know Shantoo at this camp, and he very shortly tried to leave me with an older Native American woman who was cooking the corn cakes and trading them. In his broken English, he told me he was going to trade his deer skins and would be back shortly, but for me to stay with the woman. I did not like that idea, as I did not want him to leave me alone. I then begged Shantoo not to leave me alone with that Squaw!

Shantoo turned around quickly and sharply said to me, *"What did you call that woman?"* *"That Squaw,"* I said back to him. He took me by the arm and then pulled me roughly to the side. *"Please do not address a Native American woman as a 'squaw' ever again. That is a derogatory remark to call an Indian woman a squaw!"*

I wondered what had happened to his King James English? He kept switching back and forth. I knew for certain then that I had insulted Shantoo with that remark, which I had truly said in my own ignorance. I was beginning to realize just how ignorant I really was of Native American culture, all because of my wrong indoctrination. I also knew that I had to apologize to Shantoo. and so I did, *"I am very sorry, I really did not know that squaw was a demeaning word, please forgive my ignorance."* I said to him. I could then tell by his hand gesture that he accepted my apology.

Turning to look at the Native American woman again, Shantoo then left me with her. She didn't speak English like Shantoo, and she eyed me with a strange look more than once, looking me up and down disapprovingly. I am sure I had on what appeared to be strange clothing to a Native American woman-blue jeans and a blouse. She was eyeing my collar a lot from time to time, I also noticed. Making me aware of my modern day collar, I looked around and saw that most of the Native Americans did not have collars on any of their clothing. It was all buckskin. No wonder she was eyeing my collar, she had never seen one before.

This would have surely been a strange thing for the native woman to have seen close up, I am sure. The native woman finally approached me and pointed directly to my collar. She seemed to make a hand sign implying that she wanted to touch my collar. I nodded yes that it was ok, and she reached out and touched the collar. I didn't draw back, but simply allowed her to feel the material of my collar. She also walked in a circle around me, looking at how the collar was made, I am sure. I also knew she was wondering what in the world Shantoo was doing with me, a white woman who was dressed very strangely. She probably figured he was going to sell or trade me for something, I surmised.

Shantoo returned shortly and was I ever glad to see him! I was getting sort of nervous with that native woman eyeing me all the time, and especially after she had stroked my collar. However, I could tell she was not thrilled for me to be there either, watching her. When Shantoo returned, he handed her something; she nodded her head, and began to wrap up some corn cakes, which she then gave to Shantoo. He motioned for me to follow him once again. I gladly stood up from where I had sat near that native woman and fell in step after him.

He explained that we were then going to leave *"The Branch"* and head on toward his Indian village. I was surely ready to get out of that camp anyway, and was actually looking forward to the next hike. I knew that Shantoo was not going to explain any of what just happened to me, since he was in a hurry to get on our journey, and was also a man of few words.

Before we could get out of the camp, however, a greasy, grimy rotund white man, who looked to be in his late forties, walked over and stood in front of Shantoo, spitting on the ground to his side. This strange man began talking to him in a language that sounded like Spanish to me. Oh boy did I ever wish I had learned Spanish, but regrets did not do any good at that point. Shantoo shook his head no and then made adamant gestures to the man with his hands. The man looked leeringly at me at about that time, and a cold chill ran through me, as he motioned to me and then back to Shantoo. I was even more than ever ready to leave that place. Shantoo motioned for me to then follow him, and so we went on our way, not a moment too soon for me.

A short distance down the path, I asked Shantoo what that dirty, grimy white man had asked him. Shantoo told me that the man had just offered to trade one of his pack mules for me. *"A mule?"* I thought to myself, *"wasn't I at least worth a horse?"* Of course, the whole thing was an insult to me, and I then realized the state that most women in those days had probably been in. Of course, in those days, white women had absolutely no rights, were considered property, and treated much like slaves.

This made me appreciate the fact that as a woman of today, I had many rights. In today's modern times, women now have the right to vote, and to work a regular job as men do. Women can live in today's world without being subjected to the things the women in the colonial times had forced on them. Back then, white women could be bought, sold, or traded, just like slaves.

Wondering how Native American women were treated in their tribes, I reminded myself to ask Shantoo when there was enough time to do so. So many questions I had bottled up inside, but now was not the time for asking.

As we came to the edge of the camp called *"The Branch,"* Shantoo pointed toward the big main Indian footpath that led westerly, toward what is now Bamberg, SC. *"Buffalo"* he said. *"Buffalo?"* I queried. Then I remembered that the old buffalo trail had been nearby, and in fact was believed to have been where the train tracks were later laid down in Branchville, SC, and on to North Augusta. *"Yes,"* I replied, *"Buffalo!"* I could only hope that we would see a buffalo during this journey. It was no longer hard for me to imagine that real buffalo moved in herds from inland, stopping to eat and drink while following the Edisto River to the ocean.

Shantoo was walking rapidly, and I got out of breath a little. *"Why are you going so fast?"* I asked. He didn't answer, but it came to me that he must have sensed the danger in that grimy white man, and that he might try to come after us and start some trouble. God forbid that the man should try and take me from Shantoo! Surely that man didn't think he was a match for a Native American warrior, did he? I felt safe with him now, as I had known shortly after we started our journey, that Shantoo did not intend me any harm. He was just there to guide to me on my journey back in time.

I tried to get my mind off of that grimy man, and so I ventured to ask Shantoo another question. He did not like to talk very much, and I thought that if I had to be given an Indian name, it would probably be *"woman talks too much"* Still, I had to know more about this strange country I was in, and I especially wanted to know why he had called the horses *"Sky Dogs."*

"Tell me about the "Sky Dogs," I implored of him. He shook his long black shining hair, and motioned for us to stop. He pointed to a place where he saw a log that I could sit on. Shantoo sat cross legged on the ground, as I should have known that he would do. Native Americans enjoyed close contact with *"Mother Earth."* Oh I just had so many questions! One thing I was finding out for sure, is that Native Americans were not *"savages"* as I had been led to believe from the lies I had learned from those who wrote the history books.

Shantoo then began to explain to me why the horses were called *"Sky Dogs."* He said that there was a Blackfoot legend about how the first horses had come to be known. When the Indians had first seen horses, they thought they were big dogs. He then began telling the legend:

"Three people had first approached their Indian village; two Kutani men lay sick across the backs of creatures that looked like big dogs to them. To them, the creatures were as big as elk and they had what looked like 'tails of straw.' Laying across the backs of these beasts were two sick Kutani men. One beast was also pulling a travois sled, which

had a sick woman upon it. They took the three people in, but one of them died. They were ill when they had first approached the village. One of the horses ran away also. Chief Long Arrow laughed and then said, 'These are from Old Man. (meaning God or the Great Spirit) They are a gift like the elk, antelope, buffalo and bighorn sheep, they are called Sky Dogs.' Before the strange creatures came, the Native Americans had walked from 'sky to sky' or place to place using dogs to haul things, and so the horses were called 'Sky Dogs.'

I was trying to absorb every single story and bit of knowledge or wisdom that I could, knowing that I would go back to my modern day world and tell the legend of the "sky dogs," and all of the things he would tell to me.

Shantoo appeared open to a few more questions, so I just couldn't help it, I had to ask how he kept his hair so shiny. I thought I saw a small glimmer of a smile at the corners of his mouth, and then he said, "Bear oil. Kill bear and use oil from bear to grease hair" he said. He explained that they put bear grease on their hair everyday, as well as used it to cook with.

There I was, having a most excellent adventure back in time, and I just couldn't resist getting "hair tips" from the native american. "Isn't that just like a woman?" I couldn't help but think. Yes, I was enjoying this adventure for all that it was worth.

Enjoying this new found mood of Shantoo's, I knew I had better ask him about the buffalo, which I was so very curious about as well. As I had hoped he would do, he then began to tell me about how the buffalo had made the original Indian footpaths, and how the Indians simply followed the ruts and trails that the buffalo made, in order to kill them for food.

Native Americans only killed animals for food, he explained, unlike the white men who came and killed buffalo and wasted the meat. White men then came along and followed the Indian footpaths, which later became the wagon and stagecoach trails, and in my own time, cars. From Shantoo, I learned that today many of our modern highways were once the old buffalo trails. When I had first spotted Shantoo at the local boat landing near Bamberg, SC, I was on my way to find and follow the old buffalo trail that once ran near Bamberg. Now I would get to hear more about the buffalo.

He explained how the Native Americans would track the buffalo, and other small game. Many times, they would watch for a place where small game would come and lick the ground, returning often; most times near a creek or stream. This was called a *"salt-lick"* and they would then wait in the bushes, easily getting the small animals such as deer, rabbit, and raccoon for food and for skins. He explained that Native Americans did not waste any part of the animals that they killed for food, unlike the white man.

The buffalo, he explained, being much larger than the small game, and also traveling in herds, had to travel great distances to find a salt lick big enough for the whole herd. A salt lick that would have sufficed for small animals, would not have been sufficient for a whole herd of buffalo, he explained. He told how most buffalo traveled near the river, to drink along the way to the ocean. When the buffalo finally got to the ocean, they found greater and bigger salt licks, which the whole herd could use, and which was more plentiful.

I couldn't help but ask him how the buffalo knew when to go and get the salt, having to travel so great a distance along the river to get to the ocean. He replied, *"Buffalo stomach hurt,"* holding his stomach. *"Salt make buffalo stomach stop hurting. Buffalo eat until stomach stop hurting, then go home."*

I was beginning to figure a few things out now from what Shantoo had said. Putting two and two together, the buffalo ate mainly vegetable mass, and had mostly vegetable juices in their stomach, which would be very alkaline. The addition of salt would then surely stop their stomach aches.

Curious, I also asked how the buffalo knew where the ocean was located for them to go and get the salt. *"Buffalo smell ocean and salt from far distance,"* he replied. I had never even thought of such a thing, but this all interested me without a doubt.

Shantoo shifted a little and I noticed that his moccasins had a beautiful beaded design on them, and it looked as if someone had taken great care in making them. I asked, *"Who did that beautiful beadwork on your moccasins?"* *"Wife,"* he responded. *"I bet you miss her when you go hunting, trapping and trading,"* I said to him. He nodded his head meaning yes, and I felt sure that he was thinking fondly of his wife at that moment. *"Woman talks too much,"* he said and then stood up.

I noticed that we weren't headed back down the same Indian footpath we came in on, and so I wondered how we were going to proceed. It appeared obvious that we must be going by foot. I hoped it wasn't too far, because my feet were hurting from all of that earlier hiking, and I couldn't wait to rest or lie down.

I knew that I had better keep quiet though, and not bother Shantoo with so many questions, or I might risk making him mad. I decided to save my questions for later on, as long as we got to where I could lie down and get a good night's sleep.

As we went deeper and deeper into the woods again, I saw much of the same prolific game: deer, raccoons, various birds, and wildflowers all blooming. We walked through pastures and meadows, filled with those most friendly deer and other wild animals. Again, I saw the many bunches of grapes growing wild and lush, hanging from those wild grapevines.

I marveled again as we saw peach trees, but this time I was shocked to see lemon and orange trees growing wild as well. This was truly a hunter's paradise, and it is no wonder the white settlers wanted to come here, I pondered. I asked Shantoo about the peach trees, and where they had come from. He said that the Spanish missionaries had brought the seeds and planted them. I was surely learning a lot from my native american guide.

I was getting very tired, and noticing it, Shantoo motioned for us to stop once again. This time he did not make the hand sign for us to sit down, but instead pulled out the corn cake he had traded from the squaw back at *"The Branch."* *"Eat!"* he said to me, tearing the corn cake in half, and giving part of it to me. I so longed to lie down, and held both of my palms together and held them under one side of my head, making the motion of sleep, hoping Shantoo would understand that I needed to sleep.

This did not seem to phase Shantoo. *"River"* he said, *"river,"* pointing on up ahead. By this I took it to mean that the river was nearby. I then understood that I had to keep going a little farther, and so I tried to be strong and hold up as long as I could, and so we pressed on.

Finally, I saw the river just up ahead. I wondered if we were going on downriver, or to some camp nearby to spend the rest of the evening and night. I didn't relish spending the night in the woods, remembering that mountain lion. Yet, if we had to spend the night in the woods, I felt at peace, knowing that Shantoo was a friendly and honorable soul who would protect me.

We had left the dugout canoe back at the end of the other footpath, and I wondered how we were going to go anywhere except follow along the river by foot. Much to my surprise, Shantoo immediately went to a camouflaged place near the banks and began hoisting out another dugout canoe. That told me all I needed to know, and that we were going to go on farther along the river. *"I should have known,"* I thought to myself. *"At least I would get to rest a bit in the canoe while we continued on down the river,"* I thought.

Getting the canoe ready by the water, he motioned for me to get in the front, as we had done the first time we began this journey along the Edisto together. *"Here we go again,"* I thought, *"back on the Edisto."* Something then urged me to look back at the banks of the Edisto as we shoved off. I saw a glimpse of something white through the thick underbrush along the banks, and I knew that it was the "White Wolf", still traveling along with us, yet staying at a distance. The White Wolf was guarding us, just as he had said he would do.

As we traveled on down the Edisto River in yet another dugout canoe, I began asking Shantoo to tell me more about the White Wolf. Shantoo did not speak much, and only said as few words as possible when he did speak. However, he then said something that astounded me. He told me that I had seen and met the white wolf before, and that I should try and remember where and when I had seen him before. When I had first seen the White Wolf, I had a flash of a dream, but only a flash. Now here was Shantoo telling me to try and remember.

He told me to close my eyes and try to remember, once again. Finally, a vague memory began forming in my mind, and it was something about a white wolf I had seen in the woods. Yet, I couldn't quite grasp it all, and I was only on the verge of remembering. Shantoo then spoke to me and said, lapsing into King James English, *"Thee met the white wolf in a dream." "Thee was traveling in dream, white wolf was waiting there to take thee somewhere in the dream. Thee met his family in the dream too, even though thou doesn't remember it now,"* he continued.

Hmmm....I wondered as to why Shantoo would go from speaking regular English to the King James English, as he seemed to go back and forth from one to the other. However, I was more concerned about where we were going, than I was about his choice of language.

Then, all of a sudden, the dream became crystal clear in my mind, and I remembered all of it! The entirety of the whole dream just came flooding back all at once. Yes, I had met the white wolf once before, Shantoo was right. In the dream, I was concerned about my nephew and niece, who lived in another state, and I was going to see them and check on them. I had entered a forest, but at the edge of the forest, in the dream, the white wolf had met me, and I had telepathically communicated with him in the dream. He had then taken me to meet his family, deep in the woods. After he had let me meet his family, he then took me to my own family.

How could I have forgotten that dream? I also knew that Shantoo was hinting at something that I was supposed to figure out on my own, and that he wouldn't tell me. Yet, I knew better than to ask too many questions of my native american friend, by now, and I also knew that I would have to seek answers for myself. But for now, I had remembered that I had met the "White Wolf" and his family in a dream before.

I also looked forward to hearing more from Shantoo about Hernando De Soto, and I vowed that I would wait patiently for him to tell me, in his own words, all that he knew about him. All I could remember about De Soto was that in 1540, De Soto entered South Carolina from somewhere near what is believed to be Silver Bluff, SC, near the Savannah River Plant of today.

More of the history seemed to be coming back to me, and I was glad now that I had read so much local history. De Soto and his party were looking for riches, and to find and plunder the great Indian town called *"Cofitachequi,"* which some today believe to have been near Columbia, SC. They were being guided by a young Indian boy, and must have gotten lost when they came through this area, or either the guide purposely deceived them.

I remembered a most interesting part of what I had read, how De Soto wrote letters to the other Spaniards and had the letters placed in gourds, then buried at the foot of certain trees, with a note saying to dig at the foot of the tree. He then sent Indians out to scout and they came back reporting of a nearby Indian town called Himahi, which is believed to be near the city of Orangeburg, SC today, not thirty minutes distance from my residence near Bamberg, SC.

I also remembered reading in some historic records that fields of roses were found near the town of Himahi. Even strawberries were reported to have been found there. That was something one could not forget about, fields of roses with plenty of fields of strawberries growing nearby. That sure sounded like paradise to me!

I recalled that one of the branches of the old oak at the trading camp of *"The Branch"* had pointed in the direction of what is modern day Orangeburg, SC, and what is today known as the Orangeburg Memorial Gardens, which is home to hundreds of rose bushes. Was it a coincidence that the once nearby Indian village of Himahi was reported to have fields of roses, and is now the home of the Orangeburg Rose Festival? Not a coincidence, I doubted. The native american history has all but been forgotten, and I could now feel in my heart that all of this was part of the reason for my journey.

During these musings and ponderings, I went into a state of quiet reverie, as Shantoo steered us down the meandering Edisto. I began nodding off in the canoe again, and as I did I daydreamed about the Indian town of Himahi. I could see myself walking among the fields of roses, and how they must have smelled in a small soft breeze. Just imagine putting your nose close to a modern day rose, and think of the wonderful smell, and then imagine whole fields of them. In my daydream, I ran through whole fields of roses, then stopped now and again to smell their pungent fragrance.

Also, in my daydream, the scent of strawberries and roses combined; oh how heavenly that was, and must have been. Who wouldn't have wanted to stay in Himahi, that Indian village of roses?

Obviously Hernando De soto had gold and riches on his mind, however, and nothing except getting to his destination, so that he could acquire his gold and riches. He literally did not have time to *"smell the roses"* as he and his men passed through that unique Indian village near the Edisto river, called Himahi. The sad thing is that De soto missed the true riches that were right before his own eyes, as so many of us also do today. DeSoto's eyes were blinded by his lust for treasures of the earth.

I must have dozed off for quite awhile, because when I awoke, I noticed that the sun had gone down quite a bit. Suddenly, I saw a snake glide from a tree branch into the dark waters of the Edisto. This quickly brought back a memory from my childhood, when I and a childhood friend, Cheryl Campbell, actually got lost and drifted for miles in what is called the *"Big"* Edisto River. I was probably about thriteen years old, with Cheryl being a year older than I was, if my memory serves me well enough.

We were just two young girls, staying with Cheryl's mother's friend Emily. We were swimming at what is called the *"Sand Drag"* section of the Edisto River, and someone told us that there was a *"shortcut"* through the river just around the bend from where we were swimming, which was a public swimming hole. Cheryl and I had decided we would try and find that shortcut.

Thank God we were both pretty good swimmers though. We later realized, after it was much too late, that we had somehow missed that shortcut, when the river kept getting wider and wider. We must have drifted down the "big" Edisto River for hours and hours. It took a little while for reality to set in on us, but when it did, we were both pretty panicked about it at first. I kept thinking that an alligator could bite my legs, which I was kicking like crazy trying to keep afloat. Something hit one of my legs, and I got scared, not knowing what it was! Then, I remember thinking that it might be best to conserve my energy from all of the panicked kicking of my legs, and just go with the flow of the river, simply remaining afloat. I also remember realizing that I had to stop my fear of an alligator, and begin trying to survive. Cheryl was floating not too far beside me, and we just kept on floating down the Edisto.

I am not sure how long we floated down the river like that, still looking for that shortcut. It finally dawned on us that we needed to get out of the river and turn back, but we had trouble finding a good place to get out of the river. We kept seeing a few sandbars, but the swiftness of the river made it difficult to maneuver over to them in time. We finally got over in time enough to get out at a place that looked like a sandbar. I am still not sure how long we were gone, but it took us the rest of the day to walk back to Sand Drag along the banks of the Edisto.

We also had to cross small streams, and we surely crossed many of them. The underbrush was very thick, and we had to hunt a clear enough place to cross these streams, which we managed to somehow do. We saw many snakes and other animals scampering as we made our way back to where we started. We had also been bitten by mosquitoes so badly that we must have been one big welt by the time we got back.

After all day of simply trying to survive and get back, we were so exhausted. Just two young girls, thrust into an immediate survival situation, and we survived, with God's help. Being on the Edisto now with Shantoo, I couldn't help but remember those childhood memories of when my friend and I got lost in the *"Big"* Edisto River. No, this was not my first journey down the Edisto. I had been here before.

Suddenly I knew that there had been a reason for me and my childhood friend to have gotten *"lost"* in the "big" Edisto as teenagers. Could it have been that we were being taught to overcome our fears? If that was the case, we must have succeeded or we would not have survived.

Later years, I would be baptized into the Lord Jesus Christ in the Edisto River at Bobcat Landing, near Bamberg, SC, near the exact spot where I had first seen Shantoo, my native american friend. I now knew that none of this was an *"accident"* but was ordained by God.

Also, it was no accident that I and my childhood friend Cheryl had recently been back in contact with each other after all of these years. Many things were becoming much clearer to me now that I was on my journey in time along the Edisto River of long ago. The dark waters of the Ediso held a fascinating convergence of memories for me, as well as being intertwined with my past, and my future. As a twelve year old girl, I had been lost in the Edisto River, and had made it back safe and sound. Now here I was, back on the Edisto again, this time safely in a canoe, with a Native American guide.

CHAPTER 3: THE BOOK

Shantoo and I traveled for what again seemed like hours down the ever twisting and turning black river Edisto, when finally he pulled the canoe in at a small sandbar in the river. Along the way, I had noticed that there were many beautiful small sandbar beaches on the river, where the amber colored water grew shallow close to the banks, showing off its golden tea color, which came from the decaying leaves which had turned the river into a sort of *"river tea."*

As Shantoo guided us close to the shore, we saw the remnants of clams that had been eaten by the raccoons. Seeing those clams on the sandbar banks brought back, once again, that day that my friend Cheryl and I had gotten lost in the Edisto River. I quickly put that unpleasant memory behind me, knowing I was on a very different journey now.

I also didn't have to be told to get out of the canoe this time because my feet were cramped from sitting there stationary for too many hours. Avoiding the open clams along the shore, I quickly got out and stretched my legs.

Shantoo quickly hid the canoe in another *"secret"* place near the banks of the river and covered it with brush and leaves just as he had done with the other canoe.

"Shhhhh! Shhhhh!" Shantoo whispered to me, indicating this by putting his finger over my mouth, to be quiet. He then pointed in the distance for me to look. I could not believe my eyes when I saw a big herd of buffalo, many of them drinking from the Edisto River. Some were resting in the distance while the others drank, and I could see the whole herd through the trees and brush. They too did not seem to acknowledge us, just as the deer and other animals had previously done. Shantoo informed me that we would probably see them again, since they were also moving along the river towards the same destination that we were headed-the Edistowe Indian Village, on their way to the ocean. I could not imagine that I was actually seeing the buffalo, and that was a great blessing to me.

Continuing on our journey, we proceeded up what looked like a small hill. From there we traveled about thirty minutes, hiking through the woods until we came to a small clearing.

A very crude log house appeared as we crested the top of the hill, with smoke coming from the chimney. This was certainly not a Native American village or home, and I wondered just what we were doing at a white person's homestead. *"Now this is going to be very interesting,"* I thought. I concluded that this must be part of the white English settlement he had told me about. Maybe I would finally come to know why Shantoo spoke King James English.

Shantoo and I proceeded on to the home, and to my surprise, he just walked up and knocked on the door of this colonial home. A woman asked timidly from inside, *"Who is it?"* and he replied with his name.

The door burst open and the woman came out quickly, making friendly gestures toward Shantoo. She looked to be in her mid thirties, and was very pretty with very white thin porcelain English skin and very pink cheeks. She looked at me and asked Shantoo who I was. She also spoke in King James English, with Shantoo. He replied, in King James English, that I was someone he thought well of and hoped she would let us stay the night before traveling on to our destination.

She replied, *"Certainly!"* and invited us to come in. I also heard her ask Shantoo if I spoke English, and he nodded yes, with an acknowledgment of the nod of his head. She then turned to me and asked what my name was. *"Martha,"* I replied, telling her my name. *"Anne,"* she answered in return. *"Nice to meet thee,"* she said.

As much as I wanted to ask questions of Anne, my head began to nod, and seeing that I was very tired, she motioned toward some curtains that hung at one end of the room. As I opened the curtains, I saw several meager, plain beds, and I promptly lay down on the first one I came to, not even caring about anything else but resting my weary bones. As I lay down, I noticed the crumple and rustle that the bed made, and I thought perhaps it might be straw or corn husks. I didn't care either way, and at that point in the journey, it was wonderful to my weary body to simply lie down, and I finally drifted off to blissful sleep.

I was awakened bright and early the next morning, however, to the smell of something wonderful cooking. I opened my eyes, suddenly remembering where I was, and I stared at the homemade curtains near the primitive bed. I put my feet on the floor and got up, stretching and yawning, wondering what adventure today might bring.

I pulled the makeshift curtain back and saw a glimpse of Anne over near the huge fireplace, which must have covered about eight feet along the wall of the crude log cabin. I marveled that a person could have stood inside it, it was so big. Over the fire hung a huge cast iron pot, and Anne was leaning over the pot, stirring whatever it was.

She was dressed in a typical long colonial lady's dress with a full apron, and she had on what is known as a *"mob"* hat, which looked like a frilly bed cap to me. From the front of the hearth hung iron utensils for cooking in the big iron pot. I noticed she would hold her dress to the side at certain times, to keep it from falling into the fire. What would it have been like for women to have had blue jeans back then, I wondered. Instead, I knew those long dresses must have made it harder for colonial women to do their housework and gardening. Never knowing the difference, I am sure they got along fine.

I also noticed Shantoo sitting cross legged on the floor nearby. *"Thou sleepest too late,"* Shantoo said to me. I noticed that his King James English was more pronounced when he was around this Anne lady. As he spoke, I wondered about the connection he had to this family. How did he come to be so welcome in this white home of English settlers? The woman's husband was obviously away, and yet she welcomed us in this intimate way to their home? Also, she treated Shantoo as if he were family.

"'Tis time to eat," Anne said to me. She had doled out a bowl of what looked like cornmeal mush, with molasses on the side, and cider to drink. There was bread also, she indicated as she pointed to a sliced homemade loaf of bread.

The table itself was very crude, and looked almost like two sawhorses with a board set atop. I only saw two stools, and I was told that the stools were for her husband and herself or a guest to sit on. The rest of the family sat on a long hand made bench to eat. *" Isham is out of town on business, but thee can sit on his stool."* she said to me. *"Isham will return in a week,"* she seemingly apologized. I could see that she missed her husband by the sorrowful look in her eyes.

MARTHA CLAYTON BANFIELD

I proceeded to sit on the stool she had offered and ate the cornmeal mush sweetened with molasses, washing it all down with some of the cider. I was surprised to see cider for a breakfast drink, and guessing that I was from somewhere far away, she went on to say that hardly anyone drank the water, because they believed it would make them sick. She also explained that they were very fortunate to be able to have cider and ale, as many other families less fortunate than they, had to drink beer for breakfast. She also pointed out that beer was a poor person's drink, as they had nothing else.

I speculated to myself that I knew plenty of people in the area I lived in who would probably have been thrilled to have beer for breakfast. My how things had changed since colonial times. Beer was a poor person's breakfast drink back then, something that was truly astonishing to me.

I had been hungry, there was no doubt, but beer at breakfast did not appeal to me. In fact, I did not drink anything alcoholic ever.

"I want to ask you some more questions about your life, if you don't mind," I then asked Anne. "I thought thee might want to do so," she replied. "I am ready to answer thy questions, but first we must do chores," she replied. "Come along as I do them," she said. She picked up a basket then, and off we went out the door to a planted garden out behind the house.

Evidently I had slept later than the rest of the family, because four young boys and one girl were already out in the back yard, working hard in the garden, pulling weeds. *"These are our children,"* she said proudly, waving her hand at each one as she told me their names. *"That's Isham Jr., James, Charles, and John,"* as she pointed to each one in turn. They just stared at me, probably because I had on strange clothes, such as the blue jeans. *"And that is Anna,"* she gestured toward the young girl.

Seeing that all of the children were busy at their chores, Anne then motioned for us to go to the front of the log house. As we walked to the side corner of the home, which was the sunny side, she stopped for a moment to show her herb garden to me. It was nearer to the home than the regular garden, and was basically a kitchen garden, unlike the regular garden in which the children were weeding, which grew maize (corn), beans and squash.

I used herbs myself, so I was very interested in what Anne had grown in her colonial herb garden. Among the herbs she grew were also flowers. The herbs that I saw were tansy, parsley, sage, rosemary, thyme, yarrow, bee balm, mint, violet, and lavender. She explained that rosemary was known as an herb of *"remembrance"* of friendship and fidelity and was added to wedding cakes and puddings. She also mentioned that rosemary was burned in sick chambers to purify the air, and was carried and sniffed to protect against contamination during a plague. Seeing my interest in hearing about what herbs she used, she continued informing me about some of the others she used. Brides wore rosemary wreaths as a symbol of their love and fidelity, Anne explained to me. With a look of longing, Anne then told how she herself had worn a rosemary wreath on her head when she and husband Isham were married.

Anne made it known to me in no uncertain terms that lavender was a very valuable herb to have, since baths were not a regular thing to be enjoyed as they are today. In fact, I had noticed a line of herbs drying near the fire, high up on a string near the hearth, when I had awakened earlier that morning. I too, used herbs in my modern world, but I was getting a real insight into just how very valuable these herbs were in a real life situation in colonial times.

"Yes," I replied, *"I saw your herbs drying inside near the fire as I got up."* "Yes," Anne replied, *"and lavender was one of them. I put them between the clothes when I fold them, so that they will smell sweet."*

Noticing some violets growing in Anne's herb garden, I questioned her some more about her herbs. *"Why the violet's,"* I asked, *"are they just for beauty?"* "Oh no," she replied, *"I use the violets in my wash water, to scent the water!"* I could see that everything in her herb garden had a purpose, and was grown for beauty as well as practicality.

Unlike Anne, in my modern world, I went to a store and bought a sweet smelling dryer sheet that I threw into my modern washer and dryer. I also bought dish soap, which I didn't have to prepare myself. Oh, I knew there was much more coming than just this herb garden, and more for me to appreciate in relation to how much work a woman must have had to do just to keep her family in food and clean clothes in colonial times. This was not to mention all of the work that the men were responsible for.

"Let's go on to the front of the house," Anne motioned. There, setting up a spinning wheel outdoors, was an older daughter of Anne's, who smiled timidly at me as we went around the front of the home. *"We all have to do our part in making the clothes, such as spinning and then weaving the fabric,"* Anne said. *"Elizabeth is the oldest daughter, and helps spin the yarn. Elizabeth, say hello to our special guest, Martha,"* Anne said.

I heard a barely audible *"hello,"* but that was alright by me. I could only imagine what they must think of my blue jeans, much less my modern day blouse. I knew that these good colonial folks must be way too polite to broach such a subject with me, however. I also remembered reading that the colonials took great pride in learning the etiquette that was popular in England during that time frame, simply because they didn't want the English to think they were barbarians. They wanted to appear as good or better than the English, and the world they had left behind.

Leaving Elizabeth out front, Anne motioned for us to go back inside. *"Me and thee should be able to talk freely,"* Anne said to me. *"Good, because I have so many questions!"* I replied. *"For starters, I want to know how Shantoo is so welcome in your home?"* I ventured to ask.

She smiled as we went inside and promptly went behind the curtain and brought out a book. Sitting down once again at the table, she opened this big book. To my amazement, it was a Bible, but not just any ordinary Bible. I was looking at an original Geneva Bible, which was known to be one of the three Bibles that came over to America on the Mayflower.

I was in awe, seeing that this was truly a Geneva Bible. She was not in awe of it, since it was very familiar to her, but it was obviously sacred to them. *"Let me tell you the story of the book,"* she smiled and said. *"This is also the story of how my husband and I came to know and care about Shantoo, our dear friend."*

Shantoo came in the door at just about this time. Perhaps he had been listening outside, but either way, he sat down on the floor near the other side of the room as Anne began to tell the story of *"the book."*

From time to time Shantoo would smile as she told the story. *" When mine husband goes out of town on different types of business from time to time, the children and I learned to protect ourselves as best we could. One day a white man approached the house. Being a Christian, I offered something to quench his thirst. He acted very much appreciative when I brought to him a drink of cider from the house. However, he kept eyeing the house, and asked where mine husband was. I told him that he had gone hunting and would be back shortly, not wanting this man to know mine husband was gone on a long trip."*

Anne continued on with her story, *"As I went to hand the gourd of cider to him, he grabbed my arm and tried to wrestle me down and take me prisoner. He kept saying that I would bring a good price. The children picked up stones and sticks and threw them at him, but he had a firm grip on me, and I could not wrestle myself away from this strange man."*

"All of a sudden," Anne continued telling me, *"from the woods, I heard what sounded like a Native American war whoop, and sure enough, a Native American male came running through the yard and knocked the man down, who promptly got up and jumped on his horse and left. That Native American was Shantoo. As the man went to ride off, Shantoo turned to make sure that I was alright. I had the distinct impression that this Native American could have done much worse than that to the strange man, but he did not.*

"I didn't know what to think of that strange native american who had appeared out of nowhere, but I knew he had saved my life. I offered him some cider, but he refused," Anne went on to say. *"To my surprise, he spoke a very broken English to me. I asked how he had learned English and he managed to communicate enough to me, indicating that he had learned some English from the white fur traders.*

I told him my husband would be returning soon, and would be very grateful to him for saving my life, and would he return soon to meet my husband?" "Yes," he said, *"Shantoo come back to meet husband."* Then he ran back into the woods.*"

As Anne continued telling the story, Shantoo would nod his head in agreement from time to time. Anne continued on, *"Well, mine husband returned two days later, and sure enough, the day after mine husband returned, Shantoo showed up, bearing a gift of fresh killed deer. Mine husband and Shantoo promptly went outside and skinned the deer, preparing the meat so that I could then salt it down to preserve. They had saved enough venison for a meal, and we then cooked some of it up in the pot with herbs, and we all ate together that afternoon. After the meal, mine husband went and got out the Bible and laid it on the table,"* Anne continued.

"Mine husband then began reading from the book, our Bible, and Shantoo stared with eyes so round that it seemed he had surely seen a ghost! He was fascinated by seeing mine own husband read from the "book." Afterwards Shantoo asked mine husband if he could teach him to read from the 'book' too," Anne said.

My colonial friend then continued on with the story. *"Mine husband Isham told him yes, but that both he and I would teach him. From then on, Shantoo would bring small game and deer and mine husband eventually taught him to read from 'the book.' Finally, one day, Shantoo himself read from the "book" to us. I cannot explain the joy that we both felt when that happened!"*

Anne was quiet for a moment, smiling to herself. I didn't want to interrupt her moment of sweet remembrance, but I longed to know the rest of the story. Finally, Anne continued:

"After Shantoo had read to us from the "book," he said that he wanted to tell us something. He told us that he thought that our God was the same God that he and his people worshiped, only they called him Wakan-Tanka, or by a different name. Shantoo explained to us how the heart of the native american knew and acknowledged God even from the beginning of time. He explained this to us by the quote he had found in our Bible. I guess you could say by that point in time, Shantoo and his family were like family to Isham and me."

What a story that was, to say the least! So, Shantoo was her family's protector among the native americans. God was surely looking out for these good folks. Yes, I could see that there was much sisterly/brotherly love involved here; a love that did not know or care the color of one's skin or culture.

In the meantime, I longed to hold that Geneva Bible and look at it myself. Finally, daring a venture, I asked Anne if I could hold it. *"Of course thee can!"* she exclaimed, and handed it to me gently. I held it with much care, however, as I turned a few pages. After I had carefully thumbed through it, I turned to the front, where most families kept their births and deaths.

I saw that it had been written down that Anne had married one Isham Cleiton. *"Hmmm, Cleiton- now where have I heard that name before?"* I thought to myself. *"Oh my goodness!"* I suddenly realized that *"Cleiton"* was an earlier English spelling of my own maiden name of Clayton.

"Could it be an accident that Shantoo had taken me to meet white settlers whose names were "Cleiton/Clayton?" I pondered. Hmmmmm, I thought I was being taken on a journey to see my native american ancestors. I knew that I was being taken back in time, but this was really getting very weird to me.

I pressed on, asking Anne if her name was pronounced *"Clayton"*, as mine was in the modern version. She shook her head yes, that her last name was *"Cleiton"* but pronounced the same as *"Clayton."* I was astounded and wanted to know more, and to get further clarification. However, she had no idea that my last name was Clayton also.

Yes, I was putting even more pieces of this strange puzzle together. Shantoo had told me that he was taking me to meet my ancestors, but I thought he meant only my Native Amercian ancestors. But now I saw that he had taken me to meet my white English ancestors too. I then asked Anne if she would excuse me for a moment, that I needed to talk to Shantoo.

Shantoo was standing out in the front yard of the log house, and I quickly ran up to him. I called out to him very excitedly, and he immediately saw that I was what we call flustered. I was stammering and stuttering, and asked him if Anne and her family were truly my white ancestors?

You are glad to see them, right? " Shantoo said. I then explained to him that yes I was glad to see them. *"My mission was to take thee to meet thou's* ancestors. *These are thy ancestors during the colonial days, Anne and Isham Cleiton, whose people came from England as settlers to the new colony. Not many get to see what thee are seeing, and you are very privileged to get to see this.*

Yes, he was right of course. Of course he was also on a mission as well, and one that was very unusual-a mission to take me to meet my ancestors. Of course, I had already decided that if this were a dream, I was going to enjoy it no matter what, as long as it didn't turn into some sort of nightmare.

I commented to Shantoo that Anne didn't seem to know that I was her ancestor, so obviously he had not told her who I was. Shantoo told me that she didn't need to know, and that it was only important for me to know. Shantoo and I then went back inside to Anne, who was still holding *"the book."*

I apologized to her for abruptly leaving, and she smiled sweetly, dismissing it. I asked to hold the book once again, and she handed it over to me, taking much care of it. She told me to look into the back of the book and take out the paper there. I turned to the back of the book and did as she had said.

To my surprise, it was the Cleiton/Clayton Coat of Arms. It was actually the same one that even now hung on my family's wall in modern times, but of course I knew that I couldn't tell her that. *"Should I tell her who I am?"* I thought. *"Should I tell her that I am her great grand daughter of ten generations in the future?"* In the end, I knew I could not tell her, especially if she had not guessed, and she had not.

I felt sort of like the main characters of the movie *"Star Trek"* who could not tell the mortals that they were from a future time. So, I remained quiet, until we left later that afternoon.

I had so wanted to meet her husband Isham, who was also my ancestor, but Shantoo and I could not wait as long as it would have taken for him to have returned, and I knew that we had to continue on with our journey to his own Indian Village, somewhere farther down along the Edisto.

But what about the Cleiton/Clayton coat of arms I had seen? That was pretty awesome, I had to admit. It was thought that our Cleiton ancestors in the new world had brought the heraldic Clayton coat of arms first to Virginia, and then on to the south as they spread out. I was veritably awed to be a part of this most incredible journey back in time.

As Shantoo and I later walked away from the little log house that belonged to my ancestors, Isham and Anne Cleiton, I began wishing that we didn't have to leave so soon. *"I wish we could have stayed longer,"* I said to Shantoo. *"I wanted to find out more about them,"* I said sadly to him.

Shantoo replied, *"I know you wanted to find out more about them, but we must hurry on to my village. We will camp overnight at my hidden camp on the river, then go into my village tomorrow. I am only allotted so much time to show you these things."*

He was right, of course I wanted to know so much more about it all, but I knew Shantoo was not going to tell me very much. Traveling with him, I had learned that it would all reveal itself soon enough, and not to ask too many questions.

MARTHA CLAYTON BANFIELD

CHAPTER 4: BLACK WATER

Again, just as before, I followed Shantoo as we back tracked down to the dugout canoe we had left covered up and hidden along the banks of the Edisto. He quickly found it as we went downhill to the river. We went on our way quickly, and I noticed an urgency about him that was not there before. I took my usual seat in the front of the canoe as Shantoo rowed us out toward the deep river to catch the current.

Five turtles were sunning themselves on one log as we rowed out from the banks, and it was quite a site to see. Two of them slipped into the water as we floated nearby.

I began thinking back upon the incredible things I had seen thus far in my strange journey down the Edisto river with Shantoo, my Native American guide. *"Who would ever believe me?"* I thought to myself, smiling. Oh well, even if no one believed me, I felt sure that there would be some who would.

Also, there was much mystery surrounding Shantoo, and I was surely planning on asking him some serious questions very soon. First of all, I wanted to know why I was here in this dream vision, or whatever this was. Of course, he had told me that I was to meet my ancestors. But what did that really mean? I could only venture to understand, and I continued to suspect that it might have something to do with my own fascination with Native Americans.

I had long delved into Native American history, and I just chocked it all up to that. Oh well, I sighed to myself, and then began enjoying the beautiful, serene Edisto with all of its incredible beauty. We were soon coming into an area which made an enclosure of sorts over the river, with its tree limbs. Spanish moss hung from the trees, much like a woman's hair hanging down, and I felt as if we were going through a mossy "tree tunnel." I reached my hand up and could actually touch some of the Spanish moss as we glided through.

So many different questions were running through my mind. *"Why are the animals no longer here like I am seeing in your time Shantoo? What happened to them?"* I asked. He replied, *"Remember what I told you before-white man hunted them, and unlike the Native American, the white man killed for sport, not food."* Sadly, I had to agree with him, because I knew it was true.

"Why am I here with you Shantoo, that is what I really want to know?" I asked. *"I see what the white man has done to this beautiful land called*

America, and which you call "Turtle Island" but what can I do about what has already happened?"

Shantoo replied, "You are not on this journey just for me to show you the damage that has been done, but you do have a mission also, just like I do. Who do you think called the elders together to decide on this mission of yours?" Shantoo asked. I ventured a guess and said, "The Great Spirit-God?" "Yes, the Great Spirit summoned you as well as many others, for this journey and you will know more about what your own mission is before the end of this journey," Shantoo said.

We continued on down the river, twisting and turning with the lay of the riverbed. I knew the river had changed its course through the years, and the Edisto I knew today, in 2017, was not the exact same Edisto of yesterday, since the river must have cut a new path due to erosion.

"What is the name of your indian village, Shantoo?" I asked. "It is called Edistowe Towne", he said. "You will see it tomorrow. First we go to my camp." he stated. "Tell me how you know the white people so well, please," I queried, hoping he would be open to talking at that time.

Shantoo then began to tell an incredible story, and I listened eagerly as he continued to steadily steer us downstream on the black waters of the Edisto. While smoothly steering, he told me how the Edisto Indians had been very friendly to the first English settlers, in particular to a Captain Filemon, whose ship he had entered to summon them to come to Edistowe Village. Shantoo had even guided Captain Filemon and some friends to go back to his indian village to meet the "cassique", (the chief of the Edisto Indians) at the "cassique's" request of course.

According to Shantoo, after they had been to the Edistowe village, and Captain Filemon had met the "cassique," Shantoo had guided Captain Filemon to other indian villages also.

Wow, I thought to myself. Addressing Shantoo again, I said, *"How did you get to have such authority in your village, and to be the "ambassador" to the white men?"* He just smiled and said *"Because I spoke the white man's language better than anyone in my village. Remember Isham and Anne Cleiton taught me to speak and write English correctly?"* he said and then smiled.

Shantoo went on to explain further, *"The Cassique (Chief) made me "Captain" over the whole village after he saw I could speak the language of the white man and had wisdom and knowledge to lead our village. I began to explain to the whole village that we could be friends with the white men, and that not all of them broke their promises and cheated us in trade for furs. That was what I had learned from Isham and Anne Cleiton, your white ancestors."*

It finally became clear to me and I began to see that my Native American guide was not just a regular indian scout, but was the prestigious *"Captain of the Edisto"* indian village.

I knew a little about the modern day Edisto Island, which people in my day and time called *"Edisto Beach."* Also, I had been to Edisto numerous times, but all that I really remembered about it was the many oyster and sea shells that cut your feet on your way to the beach. I finally surmised that Shantoo's "Edisto Towne" indian village must be what is known as today's Edisto Island, or Edisto beach.

I knew that I was going to soon be visiting Shantoo's *"Edisto Towne"* indian village, but tonight we would be camping at Shantoo's secret hideway or camp somewhere near the Edisto. His story about being the *"Captain of the Edisto"* indian village made me feel much more secure about him, and I no longer feared my Native Amerian guide at all.

Soon enough, Shantoo was aiming our dugout canoe for a small sandy bank along the Edisto. I knew that we would soon be heading to his secret camp. Once again, we got out of the canoe, and he hid the canoe in the underbrush and twigs. He sure knew how to camouflage something, I thought to myself. I knew we would be safe and secure spending the night anywhere Shantoo took us, and I heaved a big sigh of relief. I was suddenly very tired and looked forward to some much needed rest, but we had to get to our destination first.

We began to walk through the underbrush, and it looked as if we were on yet another small animal footpath. We hiked a good way, and I heard another of those strange piercing screeches, like the one I had heard before when I had found that arrowhead earlier. *"That sounds like another eagle screeching, Shantoo!"* I exclaimed. He just nodded his head. I began looking up, as we came to a small clearing in the heavy underbrush.

Sure enough, above us soared a majestic eagle in flight. Taking note of this, I pondered to myself that this was the second time I had seen an eagle while on our journey. Might this be the same "Great Eagle?" No sooner had I spoken that out loud, Shantoo nodded his head yes, indicating that it was truly the same "Great Eagle."

My foot suddenly struck something that felt hard, and I bent down to clutch my foot and look at it. As I gazed down at the ground, there was another small piece of flint sticking out of the ground, just like the time before. Sure enough, I dug out yet another arrowhead, in pristine shape. Putting two and two together again, it seemed to me that each time I had heard the eagle cry out or screech, I had found yet another arrowhead. Something was definitely going on, but I wasn't sure exactly what. I decided to ask Shantoo.

I asked Shantoo why each time I saw an eagle and heard it screech, had I found an arrowhead? He just smiled and told me that I had to figure out the message in it, and that it would not be right if he told me the message. Yes, of course, it was obvious that he knew, but it was not for him to tell me, I had to figure it out on my own. Well, figure it out I would do.

Shantoo once again, as with the first arrowhead, motioned for me to put the second arrowhead in my blue jean pocket, and I did just that. Wow, I now had two very awesome arrowheads in my possession! I just hoped that they wouldn't disappear when I had to go back to reality, or the year 2017.

We got back in step on the small animal footpath, taking it up again as we crossed the open field. Finally coming to yet another wooded area, Shantoo went to a certain tree and began digging in the ground to the right of it. He pulled out some items rolled in deer hide and I knew they must be our supplies for the night. He soon began making a small *"lean to"* for us to sleep under. Gathering palmetto swamp palm fronds, he put one layer on top of the other for our roof; all on top of some fallen limbs he had gathered. He had created one *"lean to"* for me, and a separate one for him, near by.

He had also spread out deer hides under each lean to, and I quickly laid down on mine, with a great big sigh. I had been ready to stretch out and relax, and I didn't hesitate getting to that deer hide quickly. It was just getting dark, and he brought out some dried deer jerky, which we ate for our supper, and I then went promptly to sleep. Shantoo had made a small fire, and I felt safe and secure.

Sometime in the night, however, I awakened to hear more growling, and I assumed it was probably either a panther or mountain lion again. I knew they would be more dangerous at night though. Shantoo was already up and creeping towards the sound. I heard some running and underbrush crackling, and I saw Shantoo running after some animal. He came back and said it was a panther, but the danger was now gone.

I lay nervously for awhile, but he told me to go back to sleep, that he would watch for any animal or predator that might come our way. I knew this Native American warrior was very adept at hunting and living off the land, and I tried to tell myself that if I would be safe with anyone, it would be Shantoo. So, back to sleep I went, with thoughts of eating bunches of those wild grapes I had seen earlier hanging ripe on the vines.

Later, I was rudely awakened by Shantoo shaking my shoulder with his moccasined foot. *"Get up!"* he said, *"you soft and lazy!"* he exclaimed with a twinkle in his eye. He handed me some more deer jerky, and I assumed that we were in a hurry to get to his indian village. Since we were in a hurry, we did not cook, but just ate the deer jerky, while gathering our things to get to the canoe, and back on the river.

When we were safely back on the black water of the winding Edisto, I began to relax somewhat, but underneath I could feel an undercurrent of suspense, since today was the day I would be taken to his indian village, *"Edisto Towne,"* as he called it.

So many questions I wanted to ask him still, but I knew that many of them would have to wait. Shantoo kept up the repetitive side to side steering, as I watched the river and the banks for wildlife and other things to amuse myself during the journey.

When he finally began talking, my ears were ready and eager to hear all that he had to say. After all, I knew he did not talk much, and so I was all ears.

"You have many dreams and visions in the night?" Shantoo asked me. *"Yes, I do."* I replied back to him. He began to explain to me that he knew that many of my dreams had been about the future of my country, the USA. *"Yes,"* that is right Shantoo," I said. *"I have had many dreams of terrible things coming to our nation if we keep going the way we are going."*

Shantoo then replied, *"That is why I am here now, on this journey with you,"* he said. *"It was prophesied in your own book, the Bible, that in the last days the Holy Spirit would be poured out on all people, men and women, and that many would dream dreams and see visions, in Acts 2:15,"* Shantoo replied, quoting from the Bible. He also said to me, *"You are just one of many who have been given a "last days" mission."*

I still could not get over a Native American warrior quoting the Bible. It was almost too incredible for me to believe, but I had just seen it with my own eyes. Ah ha, I thought to myself, now we are going to get to the heart of the matter, and why I was taken on this journey. I sat up straight and listened even more eagerly as Shantoo continued on.

He began speaking and said to me, *"You have seen the beauty of how this country used to be, while you have been on this journey with me down* the Edisto River. You have seen how the wildlife and game were once so plentiful and unafraid of man. You have seen how huge the trees used to be, and how much of a paradise it once was. You were taken on this journey so that you could see just how it used to be, and to also see how far mankind has come since the 1600's, which is the time we are now in while we are on this journey. You even got to meet some of your own white ancestors on this journey back in time. "

Shantoo continued on, "You are changed forever now. You now know more about your particular mission. You must go back and tell by writing in a book, what danger mankind is in, and give a warning to your own people. Yes, there are many people warning others in these last days, but that is your mission also, to tell them, and write it in a book, because you are a "watchman," as many are in these last days. However, you are known to us as a "scribe."

Remember that your own people, the Isham Clayton's-taught me how to "speak" or read from the white man's book-the Bible. I was delivered a sacred trust and mission through YOUR own people, and now I have been sent to deliver a sacred trust to YOU, from my own people. Your mission is in words, and writing the story so that all must know and take heed before it is too late."

Of course, I had a few questions by the time Shantoo told all of this to me. I had always felt that I had a special mission, but it was never as clear to me as when it was explained to me by Shantoo.

I was even more confused than ever by the fact that a Native American was telling me about my mission in the last days, and it was my very own white ancestors who had helped clarify his own mission. I couldn't help but think of the beauty of the way the Creator had arranged all of that, the mingling of the Native American and white man's ways to get the message out. I felt in my spirit that it was (God) the Creator who was trying to show us that we all need each other.

Shantoo began talking once again, and I listened ever so alertly to his words now, which had already revealed so much to me. He spoke once again and said to me:

"There is something else you must know. My own people, the Native Americans, had their land taken from them by your people, and many died on the "trail of tears" because of the white people. If your people of America today don't turn back to the Creator, in repentance, they will have their land overtaken also."

Staring straight ahead, Shantoo said, *"Once I did not know any better either, until your ancestors taught me how to read "the book" the Bible. Then I realized what was wrong, and why it later happened that your people took over the land and ruled us. Many of your white ancestors did not honor the true God who created all of this beautiful land that was given to us, and because of lies and greed, did not respect the land or its inhabitants."*

"I know this is true, Shantoo," I replied, *"but all I can do is apologize for what my white ancestors*

did to your people." Shantoo then said to me, *"It is good that you feel remorse or pain about what was done, but your telling your own people now is the most important thing."*

Continuing on, Shantoo explained, *"The land was given to us but evil was allowed to come in and overtake our land.* Shantoo said, *"The thing is that your own people in the United States today are also going to have the same thing happen to them that happened to us Native Americans, if they don't turn back to the one true living God."*

Beginning to hear an even sadder tone in Shantoo's voice, I sensed that he was about to end our conversation. With a heavy sigh he said, *"So, that is part of your mission, to help open the eyes of those who are blind and do not see, by telling them the truth of what will happen to them, if they do not turn back to God, through Jesus, God's son, and stop worshiping false gods and religions."*

"I will tell them Shantoo, I will tell them even louder than I ever did before." I said very earnestly, my heart heavy then with the pervasive sadness. Shantoo turned to me and with a terrible expression of sadness on his face, said, *"I know you will tell them, that is why I am here, and this is why you are on this journey."*

Knowing that I was nearing the end of my journey with my Native American friend, I still wondered why I was being taken to Shantoo's Indian Village which he called "Edistowe." Oh, well I knew I would find out the next day, and so I fell into a deep and sweetly sound sleep.

That night, I dreamed of white wolves, eagles flying and butterflies swarming everywhere. It seemed that they all were compressed into one dream. In the dream, it seemed that I might have known something very profound, but forgot it as soon as I awoke.

MARTHA CLAYTON BANFIELD

CHAPTER 5: EDISTOWE VILLAGE

The next day, after what seemed like a very long time of meandering down the Edisto River, Shantoo finally pulled our canoe off into what looked like a small creek with marsh grass growing on the sides of the creek. Thank goodness the tide was out, because I knew we could not easily wade through the marsh. Along the sides of the marshy creek which we were paddling along, I noticed many oyster banks, with small piles of oysters beside many of them.

After rowing a good way down the creek, he pulled the canoe over and gestured for me to get out. In my line of vision, past the marsh grass, was a great expanse of very large live oak trees in a field beyond the marshes. Shantoo then picked up a small rolled up hide type package from the canoe and motioned for me to get out and follow after him, through the marsh. I was so excited to finally see his indian village, *"Edistowe Towne"* as he called it, that I did not care if I got my feet wet in the marsh or not.

Shantoo reached down into a clump of marsh grass, and pulled up a strange root. He gestured to the root, and then explained to me that this was a root that the women in the village used to make their bread.

We then began to wade through small pools of standing water until we got to higher ground, and the higher ground eventually turned into a big beautiful spacious meadow with the most gorgeous yellow wild flowers. The scene almost took my breath away it was so beautiful.

I could also faintly hear the ocean from that area of high ground, and so I knew the Atlantic was close by. My spirit sensed that I was about to finally see his indian village, and I could hardly wait. I didn't know exactly why my spirit had leaped so much in anticipation of this event, but nevertheless, it had.

Before we moved on, Shantoo held his hand up, gesturing for me to stop. I didn't mind at all, since the meadow was so beautiful to behold. As we both stood very still, Shantoo pointed in a specific direction, and I gazed at the most amazing sight. Across the meadow was a very big cluster of butterflies, all seeming to come out of a wooded area, fluttering out into the open meadow. As they got to the meadow, they spread out and seemed to cover its entirety. It was very surreal to me, and I had never seen anything like it. It looked like a glistening "butterfly blanket" to me.

There we were standing right in the middle of yet another one of the most unusual butterfly swarms I had ever seen, which covered the entire meadow. As I looked closer, the butterflies began landing on the yellow wildflowers themselves. As I watched in amazement, Shantoo held out his index finger, and as he did, a butterfly landed on it, just as if he had coaxed it to land. Yet, I knew he had said not a word. We said nothing further, and moved on along our journey, both knowing that something very spiritual had just happened. I would have usually been very vocal and talked excitedly about the butterflies, but there was a sacred solemnity that seemed to permeate the air. For perhaps the first time ever, I actually had no words. It seemed almost sacreligous for me to have spoken, and so I remained quiet for some time afterward; that is, until we actually entered "Edistowe Towne."

When we finally entered Shantoo's village called "Edistowe," the first thing I laid my eyes upon was a great round type house, which was obviously considered a sort of "state" house. Shantoo led us to the entrance of this house, where I saw an elevated or high seat, considered to be a throne, where the "cassique" or chief sat, with his wife at his right hand. This chief or "cassique" himself was an older, very large man. The elevated platform looked to be able to seat about a half dozen persons. On lower benches surrounding this elevated platform on both sides, were seated men, women and children.

In the center of this "round" house burned a continual fire, with small low furrows surrounding it. I was then taken and seated beside the cassique's wife, on one side, and presented with skins, or animal hides, as a welcoming gift, I supposed.

I was even more excited than normal because I knew that "Edisto" village had been the main destination on this journey, and I could only imagine seeing this indian village for myself. Of course, I had read historic accounts about "Edistowe Towne" but it would surely pale in comparison to actually getting to visit. Still not exactly knowing how it was possible, there I sat beside the wife of the great "cassique" himself, chief of "Edistowe Towne."

In what I was to learn later was a *"welcoming"* ceremony or gesture, the Indians began welcoming me by stroking my shoulders with their palms, while sucking in their breath at the same time. It made me wonder if they were actually trying to *"smell"* me or get my scent, so to speak. It seemed a very strange way to welcome strangers, in my way of thinking.

Sitting there beside the chief's wife, I remembered the amazement I had when we first walked up to the round house. What looked to be rows of elm trees were planted on either side of the very large, spacious entrance to the house itself. I learned later on that the men of the village, with six foot staves in hand, ran two by two, after a marble bowl which is thrown out randomly. The object of the game was to see whose stave got closest to the bowl. The winner would then win beads as the prize. In this way the men of the village exercised themselves mainly during the winter months. It appeared too violent for my liking, however. Also, before we entered the *"round"* house, I noticed a small area for children of the village to play.

While sitting inside the *"round house"* at the side of the great Cassique's wife, I recalled gazing out on huge growing fields of corn or maize, with Indian dwellings or homes dotting the fields of maize. The Spanish, according to Shantoo, had rediscovered Edisto Island, and so began planting crops.

I wondered at the life of the women of this village. What would a day have been like in their lives? I do know for certain, after this journey I had been on, that these native americans did not damage the earth like the white man had done. They knew that if they abused mother earth, they would pay a price.

Shantoo explained to me that oysters were plentiful and eaten by everyone in the village. After eating all of those delectable oysters, some of the young boys came and gathered up all of the shells, and took off with them. Shantoo informed me that they were going to dump them in a certain location, which is today, in my time, known as the *"Edisto Shell Ring."* Shantoo also informed me that the shell deposits or "middens" had been there a very long time, even since about 4000 years ago.

It is strange how something that was done in such a matter of fact way back then, was later considered a complete mystery. Modern archaeologists still speculate if the shell rings were ceremonial or simply the oyster dump. Right now, all I cared about was getting on with our journey.

Later that day, as the sun began going down, we were summoned to a great feast that appeared to have been prepared in our honor. There was a great long table of foods I was unfamiliar with, and yet Shantoo had informed me to try and eat some of it, or the Chief would be greatly insulted. That was the hardest part of all, eating things and not knowing if I was eating raccoon, possum, bird, deer or even things that might creep in the night. Yet, I was glad to be there and so I ate.

At the end of the meal, some of the Native Americans began beating their drums lowly at first. To my amazement, the chief's two daughters came forth, dressed in Spanish moss type wrap gowns, interwoven with beautiful colored beads. That is the best way I can describe what they were wearing. They then did a sort of sacred religious type dance, and afterward presented themselves to Shantoo and me, standing directly in front and facing us, as if waiting for our approval. Shantoo nodded to them as if in thanks.

Shantoo told me later that only the Chief's daughters or wife were allowed to wear the Spanish moss ceremonial dresses, since in my world they were similar to gowns which could be worn only by royalty. Shantoo explained that this meant great respect to a guest to have this dance done in their honor.

At the end of the dance by the chief's two daughters, they then left but came back quickly, holding a kind of Spanish moss shawl between them both, decorated in many colored beaded designs interwoven in the moss. They walked over to their mother, the Chief's wife, and as the drums got louder and louder and began pounding more rapidly, the Chief's wife stood as her two daughters came before her with the Spanish Moss type shawl.

As she stood, they draped the shawl type moss around the neck of their mother, and the drums came to a crescendo of volume as the shawl was placed upon her. I then understood that it was a type of queenly "stole" that they were putting upon their mother, which also showed her "rank" in the tribe, as over all the other women. She wore it proudly too, turning to each side so everyone could see. When it was fitted upon her just right, the drums died down, being played at lower and lower volume, and they slowed down in pace considerably. The daughters then backed away out of sight, and the drums sounded no more. The Chief smiled broadly, proud of his wife and daughters.

Shantoo later explained to me that only women wore the Spanish moss, many times as ordinary dresses in the summer when it was hot. However, he said that on special occasions the women liked to show their rank in the village by wearing their ceremonial Spanish moss gowns. Shantoo once again reminded me that only the chief's wife or daughters could wear the ceremonial gowns.

Shantoo also explained how the women harvested the Spanish moss, boiling it to get the chiggers out, then drying it and using it for several different purposes. In my own time today, I had thought of selling our southern spanish moss at one time to northerners, but couldn't figure out how to get the chiggers out-but now I knew! As I was told, one such purpose for Spanish moss was as a sort of baby diaper, (when braided) women's feminine pads, and also as a drape over poles to create shade.

This appeared to me to be similar to women being known as seamstresses or the ones who made the clothes in our society. Anyway, it was a woman's job to work and use the Spanish moss. In their tribal society, it was women who wore the Spanish moss, also called "Tree Hair" by the native americans, or "hair of the tree."

When this ceremony was over, Shantoo led me over to a middle aged native woman, who then took me to a place where I was to sleep, in her own family dwelling. I thought to myself, *"Sleep? How can I sleep after all of this excitement of being in Shantoo's Indian village of Edistowe Town?"* There was just no way I could easily go to sleep.

Trying to process all that I seen in the Edistowe Village so far was hard enough to do, but the unknown mystery of the whole trip was something else altogether. Everything in this journey had an element of suspense and surprise, which did not make it easy for me to fall asleep. Thoughts kept going back and forth in my head. Finally I fell asleep, but not after a good while.

After awakening the next morning, Shantoo informed me that he wanted me to meet someone. He immediately took me to an elderly Native American woman. While speaking his own native language to her, he also gestured towards me as he was by now fond of doing. He then turned to me and said, *"This lady is your ancestor, and she will take you with her today and talk with you. Be sure and listen carefully to all that she has to say to you because you will learn much."*

Well, I was glad that Shantoo hadn't sprung that one on me like he did with my white English ancestor, Anne Cleiton! At least this time I would know in advance who this lady was.

This elderly Native American woman looked to be in her seventies. Her hair was gray and had been braided into a long braid. Surprisingly however, she could walk without help and seemed very spry for her age. She indicated through hand signs that I was to follow behind her.

She arose from where she was sitting and waved with her hands for me to get in line behind her as she began a trek along a narrow footpath that led away from the village. Normally I would not have immediately done what she said, but I had come to explicitly trust my native friend Shantoo.

I came to realize that this old woman seemed to be heading toward the ocean itself. That was just fine with me, to say the least. The narrow path was just wide enough for one person, and I easily kept up with the old woman's pace. As we came closer and closer to the ocean, I could smell the salty smell of the ocean air even stronger.

"I want you to see something," spoke the old woman in a sweet voice. As we drew closer to the ocean, I could see that we were gazing upon a most special and sacred site. There along the beach, was a herd of buffalo, licking the salt off of the sandy ground. It occurred to me that it could have been the same herd of buffalo that I had seen with Shantoo earlier. Some of the buffalo were licking the salt in a few of the marshy depressions also.

"The buffalo have now all but disappeared, just like our native people," she continued on. "You are seeing how they once were, and we know that Great Spirit gave them to the Native Americans to sustain us and for food."

The old lady kept speaking, "Your journey down the Edisto has come to an end now. You have met your white ancestors, and now you have met your Native American ancestors here at the Edistowe Village. Your white ancestors from long years ago no longer exist, but their ancestors live on today.

Also, your native ancestors, the Edistowe Indians, have become extinct, and no longer exist. Our people have suffered much, but we still live on in the heart of the Great Spirit, and a remnant of our people."

The old woman continued on: "Do not forget the animals that you have met on your journey down the Edisto River. You may meet some of them again. When your vision of the future falters, the eagle might show himself to you again. When you might be in danger, or forget your way, the white wolf might appear to you in person, or in a dream. He will help you find your way, or keep on course, as he has done before.

The butterflies you will continue to see, and will be a sign to you that your Creator is with you. Never forget that!

Your Creator has been speaking to you the whole time, but it is only in the past ten years that you really began to notice and have begun deciphering what He was saying to you.

You are no longer that eagle on the ground, you are the eagle soaring above. You have fought many traps and disguises which the evil one put in place for you, and it is only because of the grace of our Creator God that you have escaped the evil ones clutches. You will now help others escape the delusion too.

The little girl that you once were, whose young heart was abused and shattered, has now been healed. This journey was her journey also.

When Jesus was on earth as a man, He knew how much His Father in Heaven loved Him. You now also know how much your Father in Heaven loves you too, because He sent His only Son to die for you and all of mankinds sins. Go in peace now and write down all that has been shown to you on this journey."

As the old woman stopped speaking, I suddenly heard a rustle in one of the trees nearby, and turned my head to look in that direction. As I turned back to look at the old native woman, she was gone, just simply gone, just like that!

As I turned back again to the tree where I had heard the rustling sound, I then saw a beautiful white owl, taking flight. I had the strangest feeling that the owl was the old woman.

Unsure what to do next, I looked once more at the herd of buffalo licking the salt, and then turned and slowly began my way back to the village. On my way back, I once again saw the Great Eagle, screeching high above me. As I looked up, once again, I knew what the eagle was going to do. He then flew down to the footpath that I was on. Then, right in front of me, he dropped something from his beak, and flew away.

Yes, it was another arrowhead that the Great Eagle dropped right in front of me, which now made three arrowheads that I had been given. The Great Eagle then flew off, just as the white owl had done.

Returning back to the village on the same path I had first came on, I saw Shantoo walking toward me on the same path. Shantoo looked at me and then said, "My mission with you has ended, just as the old woman's mission has ended with you. You know what to do now.

You will go back and write a book of all that you have seen and all that we have told you. I will see you again someday, but I do not know when.

You will know it is me when you see me, that is all that I can tell you."

MARTHA CLAYTON BANFIELD

Chapter 6: Waking Up

I was gently roused from what seemed like a blissful sleep by the smell of bacon and eggs. Turning over in my bed, trying not to smell that enticing aroma of bacon, I then remembered the vivid and surreal dream that I had dreamed, about being taken back in time by a Native American warrior. Wow, what a dream it was-one of those that just seem SO real! I just wanted to go back to bed and continue the dream, but my husband James walked into the room, urging me to get out of bed. The smell of bacon then permeated the entire room, and I knew there was no going back to bed then.

"I have cooked you breakfast. Get up and eat!" James said as he came into the bedroom, the smell of bacon seeming to follow him.

"I had a very strange dream James!" I exclaimed. He said, "you always have strange dreams, hon!" "No, this one was different, very different!" I replied to him. I urgently wanted to tell him about it and so I continued on describing in detail my strange dream, while sitting up on the side of the bed, putting on my slippers. When I got through telling him about the dream, James said that there would be only one way that I could tell if it had been a dream, or if it had been reality. "What is that?" I asked James.

James went on, "Well, if it had been just a dream, there would be no physical evidence of it. YET, if it was reality, there might be some physical evidence." I didn't understand what he meant, and so questioned him further.

James then said, "Check your pockets, check the bed, and see if you find anything strange or weird." Yeah right I thought, I said sarcastically. I then checked my pockets but there was nothing. In the dream, I had promptly put the 3 arrowheads in my pocket, which is what Shantoo had told me to do. Yet, no arrowheads, nothing nothing nothing.

Still considering that James might be right about this "evidence", I looked on the bed and saw nothing. Removing the covers off of the bed, I found nothing there either. Oh well, I did look, hoping that I might find something. It seems there was nothing to be found after all. To say that I was disappointed, would be putting it lightly. At the bottom of my bed I saw what looked like some vestiges of sand, and I quickly brushed the sand off the bed, thinking that I must have forgotten to brush off my feet before getting into bed. Finding no real "evidence" of the dream being a reality, I then gave up on that idea.

I joined James in the dining room and we ate breakfast together, still pondering the strange dream. James made a suggestion that we should ride down to Branchville, SC (aka The Branch) and then on to Edisto Beach for the day. Why not, I thought? He and I always seemed to love going on some historic adventure together anyway. We knew we could make a day's excursion of visiting the modern day places of the dream.

So, getting our things together, we got into the truck and off we went, heading to Branchville. I told James that we should at least start our excursion out the way my dream had started, at Bobcat Landing. We then drove out to Bobcat Landing, noticing that the water was very low since there had not been much rain.

Standing at Bobcat Landing, I pointed out the exact spot where in my "dream" I had seen the Native American across the landing, just off the banks of the Edisto. James said, "Wow, you describe it as if it really happened!" I knew then that I felt deep inside of me, that the dream WAS real. It was as real as anything I had ever done!

Afterward, we drove down what is left today of that old buffalo trail, which intersects Hwy. 78, where we then took a left, heading on to Branchville.

Once we got into Branchville, we searched for the modern day location of where the old oak tree was once located. Finding it, with the help of our friend Eddie, we saw the American flag flying near there with a small monument to the first settlement of the town of Branchville.

Thinking of what had transpired since "The Branch" had only been native american villages, it is amazing that Branchville SC later became the site of the world's first Railroad Junction. Branchville was also part of the world's longest railroad, which ran 136 miles from Charleston SC to Hamburg, SC. Later, in 1838, Branchville became the first railroad junction built by spliting a rail, creating a spur that went to Columbia SC. We pondered, sad to say, that not many even knew that the three Native American camps were ever there at all.

Standing there near the monument of the town, we could see into the fields off in the distance, where two of the camps were. Time rolled on, and yet there we stood, gazing out over a much different modern day landscape. Our friend Eddie also pointed out where the third native american camp must have been.

Eventually, we turned and left to go on our continuing adventure to Edisto Beach. On the way down to the beach, we stopped to buy some drinks and refreshments. While standing in the convenience store, I began digging into my pockets as I had done earlier that morning. I felt something bulky this time, and to my surprise pulled out three perfect arrowheads.

Where did they come from? Why weren't they there earlier that morning? They were the same three arrowheads I had found in the dream, I was sure of it.

Getting back into the vehicle, I excitedly showed the arrowheads to James. He simply nodded his head, reached his hands out to hold them and said, "I knew it wasn't a dream! I just knew it!"

ABOUT THE AUTHOR

Martha Clayton Banfield is a Christian Author and former newspaper columnist, Singer/Songwriter/Musican, who is based out of Bamberg South Carolina, where she lives with her husband James, 4 cats and a rabbit.

Martha has published four other books, all available on amazon.com.

For signed autographed copies of this book or any of her other books,

you can email Marty at

martybanfield @gmail.com

OTHER BOOKS
BY MARTHA CLAYTON BANFIELD

PRODIGAL DAUGHTER

HE WANTS YOUR HEART

STARVING THE DEMONS

SPREAD THE WORD